Douglas Dunn was born in 1942 in Renfrewshire and fir[illegible] worked as a librarian before studying English at Hull University. After graduating he worked in the Hull University library under Philip Larkin.

Dunn's first co[illegible] *Terry Street*, was published in 1969 and won [illegible] am Award. He became a full-time writer in [illegible] n won the Whitbread Book of the Year for [illegible] tten in response to the death of his first wife. [illegible] of English at St Andrews University in 19[illegible] dir[illegible] Director of St Andrews Scotti[illegible] r 19[illegible].

He was awarded [illegible] ueen's Gold [illegible] for Poetry [illegible] poetry are [illegible] *Parliament* [illegible] ted *The F[illegible]k of Twentieth* [illegible] *The Oxford* [illegible] *of Scottish Sh*[illegible]

Douglas Dunn was born in [illegible] in Renfrewshire and first worked as a librarian before studying English at Hull University. After graduating he worked in the Hull University library under Philip Larkin.

Dunn's first collection of poetry, *Terry Street*, was published in [illegible] and won the Somerset Maugham Award. He became a full-time writer in 1971. In 1985 Dunn won the Whitbread Book of the Year for *Elegies*, poems written in response to the death of his first wife. He became Professor of English at St Andrews University in 1991, and was the founding Director of the St Andrews Scottish Studies Institute in 1993.

He was awarded an OBE in 2003, and the Queen's Gold Medal for Poetry in 2013. Among his collections of poetry are *St Kilda's Parliament* and *Dante's Drum Kit*. He has edited *The Faber Book of Twentieth-Century Scottish Poetry* and *The Oxford Book of Scottish Short Stories*.

The Gathering Storm

LYNNE McEWAN

First published in the United Kingdom in 2024 by

Canelo
Unit 9, 5th Floor
Cargo Works, 1-2 Hatfields
London SE1 9PG
United Kingdom

A CIP catalogue record for this book is available from the British Library.

Print ISBN 978 1 80436 231 0
Ebook ISBN 978 1 80436 230 3

Cover design by Blacksheep

Cover images © Depositphotos, Getty Images, Shutterstock

Look for more great books at www.canelo.co

Printed and bound in Great Britain by Clays Ltd, Elcograf S.p.A.

1

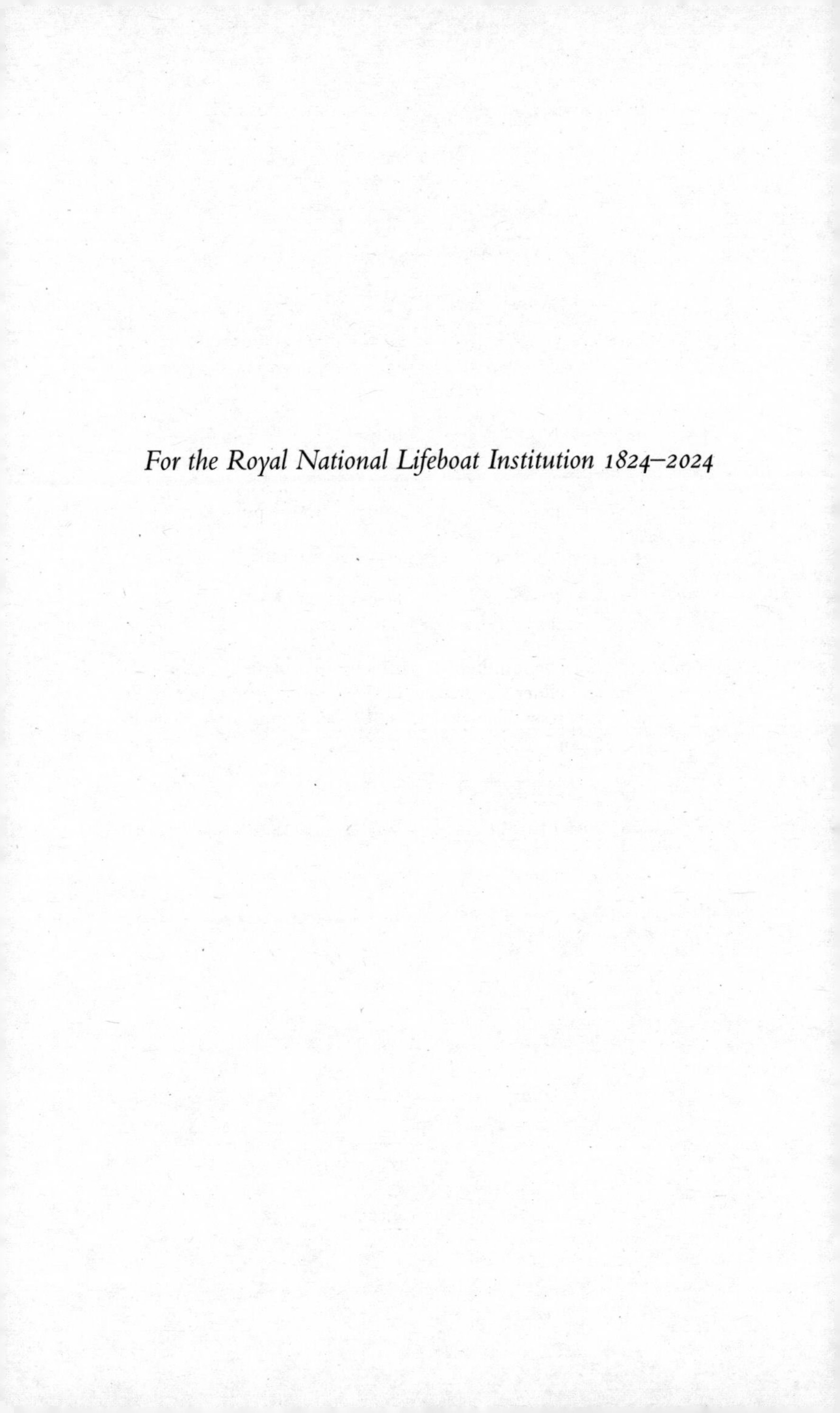

For the Royal National Lifeboat Institution 1824–2024

'With courage, nothing is impossible.'

Sir William Hillary

Chapter 1

As the taxi crossed Blackfriars Bridge, Detective Inspector Shona Oliver gazed out of the window at the Thames, and the view she knew so well. A little way upriver, the low, wooden structure of Tower RNLI station, where she'd begun as a lifeboat volunteer, perched like a seabird's nest above the broiling brown water of a high tide. Beyond, the City of London's towers and spires pierced the thin mist, a glittering cliff face of steel and glass, pristine and dazzling in the rising sun. Her husband, Rob, in the seat beside her, smiled and squeezed her hand.

'It'll be fine,' he said, seeing the small crease of concern between her eyebrows.

'I don't know how you can be so calm,' she said, exasperated.

For nearly twenty years, as a beat cop with the City of London Police, then as a detective among its boardrooms, powerhouses and institutions, Shona had worked to keep her country's capital safe. Now, she was returning not as a member of an illustrious police force that could trace its roots back two millennia to Roman Londinium's city watch, but as the wife of the accused.

But no hint of concern about this morning's business clouded Rob's features. He looked groomed and confident, with his silver-fox hair and impeccable navy suit. Throughout the two-week trial, his certainty that the jury would acquit him on charges of money laundering had never wavered. After eighteen years of a marriage with many ups and downs, Shona regarded his perpetual self-confidence with an intense mixture of irritation and admiration.

The taxi drew up in front of the Royal Courts of Justice, known the world over for the street in which the building stood, Old Bailey. Shona stepped out onto the narrow pavement. Above her, pale stone pillars and arches the colour of old bones rose to the dome and the bronze statue of Lady Justice with her balance scales and sword. Shona's hand went automatically to her bag, feeling for her policy book, but the realisation washed over her. No evidence she could be called upon to give would change today's outcome. She reached out instead to her husband.

Rob drew her to him and pushed back a strand of her hair, the same dark brown that so precisely matched the colour of her eyes. Her straightened bob was already beginning to return to its natural curl in the dampness of the autumn morning. Shona forced herself to smile. He was right. Nothing to worry about.

Throughout the trial, she'd sat in the public gallery and scrutinised the prosecution's case. Two members of Rob's team at Milton McConnell Bank had co-mingled the legitimate transaction of a pharmaceutical company with fake client accounts, thus laundering the proceeds of criminal activity. Rob had signed off on some of the transactions before he realised what was going on. The bank, hoping to avoid a scandal, had paid him off but, when later reporting the details to the police, he'd found himself accused of masterminding the fraud. Shona had been incandescent with anger at him for keeping his suspicions from her, and putting their family and their future in such jeopardy, but the two team members involved had been duly convicted and jailed. Rob's barrister had pointed out that neither his actions, nor indeed his bank balance, supported the claim he was involved in the laundering of £26 million into gold bullion, which had apparently been smuggled abroad and recast, and was as yet unrecovered.

'Ready?' Rob said, as if she was the one about to face a jury. She nodded.

Shona went up the steps on his arm, focusing on how it would feel to finally take him home, reopen their B&B and get back to normal.

Anoushka Templeton – an old school friend of Rob's and, currently, his barrister – was waiting with her junior and a solicitor. They hugged, a kiss on each cheek. As Shona left them to make her way to the public gallery, she turned back to wave, but no one looked her way. Anoushka adjusted her wig while Rob was buttoning his suit jacket and straightening his cuffs, as if they were actors in the wings about to go on stage. For a fleeting moment, a sense of powerlessness struck Shona like a physical force, as if she'd suddenly become a mere member of the audience in her own life while key events played out in front of her, beyond her control.

Shona sat alone in the pew-like benches of the gallery looking down on the courtroom. She took deep breaths, holding them to the count of four, then slowly exhaled, straightening the front of her own dark business suit and pale pink silk blouse. It was a work outfit, appropriate for most situations a senior CID detective might encounter. She'd donned it like armour this morning, hoping to project an air of confidence she didn't feel she possessed.

It was as if she'd passed through the mirror. Shona had been a police officer all her adult life and the law was the structure that underpinned that life. Now she was forced to watch it at work on one of the two people she loved most in the world. The other, their sixteen-year-old daughter, Becca, had lived under the shadow of the case for months. She'd coped with it well – a mix of her mother's determination and her father's optimism, Shona thought ruefully.

She and Rob would go straight home after the verdict. This evening they'd be at High Pines, all three together. They'd stand at the floor-to-ceiling windows above that glorious estuary and resolve not to look back at this difficult time. The future was all that mattered.

In the dock, Rob settled himself then grinned up at her. The jury appeared relaxed as they filed in. That was good, Shona told herself. It meant they were of one mind. English law weighed in favour of the defendant – innocent until proven guilty – and in her experience the average juror took the judge's direction to heart: *you must be convinced beyond reasonable doubt.*

And *doubt* was the key word. They wanted forensics, witnesses, clear evidence of wrongdoing and, in Rob's case, that was circumstantial or absent. And the psychology of juries meant that members were often more concerned about jailing an innocent man than setting a guilty one free. To mistakenly incarcerate a blameless individual would play on their conscience. However, freeing someone who later reoffended just meant the police hadn't done their job properly building the case, and therefore that was the constabulary's fault. Then there were those jurors who just didn't trust anything the police said. The irony wasn't lost on Shona. She'd seen juries acquit before and had always cursed them for it. Now, here she was praying Rob would benefit from just such a set of circumstances.

The judge asked the foreperson to stand. The woman, with her smart green cardigan, erect posture and precise movements, looked competent and efficient.

In the dock, Rob fixed his eyes on the royal arms carved on the judge's bench. Shona felt a surge of pride that he'd come forward and admitted his own unwitting part in the fraud. The proceeds of organised crime fuelled further waves of human misery – the drug trade, human trafficking and prostitution – and he'd done his duty in taking a stand against it. Rob's career in banking was over, even with the jury rubber-stamping his innocence, but she didn't see that as a problem. Running their well-reviewed boutique B&B on the Solway Firth allowed his sociable and creative side free rein. They had debts and their marriage had been rocky at times, but she had no doubt they'd make it a success, once the trial was behind them.

'Have you reached a verdict upon which you have all agreed?' the judge said. His expression was benevolent, encouraging the forewoman to speak loudly enough to be heard by the entire court.

'We have, Your Honour,' the woman replied.

'Do you find the defendant guilty or not guilty?'

'Guilty.'

Rob put a hand on the rail of the dock to steady himself.

In Shona's ears, the sea rushed in. Rob turned and raised his head to the public gallery. It was like he was already being swept away from her. She'd seen that look of shock and bewilderment on the faces of the drowned just before the water closed over them. *I love you*, he mouthed. Then was gone.

Shona stared at her hands clasped in her lap, knuckles white. She replayed the verdict like a tape, over and over, praying she'd somehow misheard. By the time she looked down at the court again, the jury had been discharged, and the judge and barristers and clerks were filing out. It was all over. Mechanically, Shona stood up and returned to the hallway.

Anoushka was suddenly in front of her. Shona tried to take everything in, but it felt too much. Rob was going straight to prison. She only had five minutes to say goodbye. He was innocent, but jury trials were notoriously fickle. She, of all people, should have seen this as a possibility.

Anoushka led her to a discreet door on the ground floor. A buzzer sounded, and they descended a white-washed stairwell that seemed to grow greyer and greyer.

She'd been into the bowels of the Old Bailey before, but this time the institutional smell of bleach and echoes crowding from every hard surface almost overwhelmed her.

In the holding cell, Rob had taken off his jacket and looped it around his chair. To an impartial observer, it looked like a regular business meeting. Only the pallor of his handsome face and the slight tremor in his outstretched hands betrayed him. He hugged her, quickly, then pushed her into the seat opposite as the two members of the custody staff – both wearing regulation white, short-sleeved shirts and black trousers, and sporting buzz cuts – stepped forward to separate them.

'Go to my office,' Rob said urgently, leaning across the table to clasp both her hands in his. 'There's a list in my desk of the people you should call. They'll help you. The B&B owners' association. A couple of other parents of home-schooled kids who know the ropes.'

'What d'you mean there's a list?' Shona tried to pull back her hands, but he held on until she wrenched them away, her nails leaving white half-moons in the soft flesh of his fingers. 'You said everything would be fine. How could you let this happen?' She banged the flats of her hands on the table hard enough to earn a warning look from the custody staff. The thinner of the two men looked set to intervene, but her responding expression said, *don't even try it*. After a moment, he leaned back against the wall and folded his arms.

'Ask Sandy. He'll help.'

Rob's older brother had inherited the family auctioneering business, which he ran with his fearsome wife, Caroline.

'Are you kidding me?' Shona said, indignant. 'If Sandy was going to help, he'd be here now. He won't even return my calls.'

She was split in two, grasping with gratitude at his uncharacteristic foresight in putting at least some plans in place for her and Becca, should the worst happen, and fury that he'd kept doubts about his release to himself.

He gave her the charming little shrug he used when he couldn't think of an excuse for some minor domestic infringement. I used all the milk. There are guests coming at short notice. I forgot to tell you I might be found guilty.

'It will be fine. We'll appeal,' he said.

'On what grounds?' She wanted to slap him out of his insouciance. Shake him until his teeth rattled and he finally realised the very deep shit he was in. As far as she could see, no elements of the trial could be called into question on a point of law or the inadmissibility of the evidence.

'Don't worry. We'll think of something,' he reassured her.

Shona levelled a finger at him. 'Do not patronise me. Just remember who you're talking to.'

She was boiling with hurt and anger while he'd quickly regained his equilibrium, but in that moment, his expression slipped, and she saw what he was doing. In reassuring her, he was reassuring himself. For Rob, his mother's golden child, scholarship boy and university blue, life had always worked out, until now. But somewhere inside him, he still carried that luck, like a talisman that would come good with just a little burnishing.

She wanted to tell Rob she understood, but the custody officer stepped forward and this time he wasn't deterred by Shona's glare.

'Time to go.' His manner was half-priest, half-bouncer. Reflect on your sins and drink up.

Rob got to his feet. Shona stepped around the table and clung to him.

'We can sort this,' Rob breathed into her hair. 'My Shona willnae let it beat her. Look after our girl.'

Then he was gone, and the clang of doors reverberated along the corridor.

Becca, Shona thought. How would she break this news to Becca?

'What will he get?' Shona rounded on the barrister, who'd waited outside the cell to allow the couple a last moment together, but she already knew the answer. Up to fourteen years and a potential confiscation order of assets, including High Pines.

The barrister leaned against the wall, still in her robes. Her face was gently reassuring but Shona could see the concern etched beneath her carefully curated expression.

'You might have to face the fact he'll be in prison for some time,' Anoushka replied.

'This is Delfont's doing,' Shona spat. She was convinced her former boss – DCI Harry Delfont – had targeted both her and Rob after she'd started asking questions about his possible links to an organised crime group. 'He set Rob up. If I can find evidence on Delfont, how he was involved in this money laundering for an OCG, we can appeal, can't we?'

Anoushka sighed. 'We'll look at an appeal, of course, but without compelling, new evidence...'

'What that bastard did to me...' Shona shook her head. 'What he's done to Rob, he can't get away with it, he just can't.' Her bitter tears were dammed up behind a wall of anger. Any moment it might give way, and suddenly she felt like it was taking all her energy just to hold the torrent at bay.

Anoushka took her arm. Shona allowed herself to be led back to the stairs. With each step, she was climbing a mountain. The air was thin, and she thought she might faint. But gradually, with painful slowness, the light came back.

The silver-and-gold marble of the vaulted entrance hall stretched above her, the statuary impassive, the folk in the mural that ran around the Old Bailey's interior going about their business as if the world had not irrevocably changed. There she was again, Lady Justice with her blindfold, but it was Shona who should have seen this coming.

Anoushka accompanied her outside. The sun seemed unbearably bright. Shona stood with her face in her hands for a moment. The tears remained behind her eyes and wouldn't fall. Instead, she drew strength from the fury she'd felt seeing Rob in the cell. She rubbed her face, lifted her chin and shook back her hair.

My Shona willnae let it beat her.

No, she wouldn't. But how long could she go on like this?

She had no doubt that Rob loved her and Becca. He'd often told her he'd do anything for his family. He'd stood by her in the worst of times. She was convinced Delfont had set him up. But there was no getting away from the fact that Rob had made poor decisions, and now she and Becca would also pay a high price for them. She'd be the cop with the jailbird husband, her reputation under perpetual scrutiny, and Becca would be the daughter of a convicted criminal – a taint evident to every future employer, university, friend or partner who googled her.

Shit. Shit. Shit. What a mess.

The barrister was looking at her with concern.

'I'm fine, really. It's just the shock,' Shona said, as much to convince herself as to allay Anoushka's fears. 'Thank you for all you've done. I'm heading straight to the train station. You get yourself off.'

They hugged goodbye with promises to be in touch soon.

Shona had better tell Becca before she saw it on the news. Taking out her phone, she stared at the screen, formulating the combination of words that would soften the blow, but nothing would come. Eventually, she pressed the number.

'Hi, Mum.' Becca's voice sounded light and full of hope.

'I'm sorry, darling,' Shona said, as the tears finally fell.

Chapter 2

Three months later

As the Kirkness lifeboat headed out into the Solway Firth, another wave ambushed them. Shona narrowed her eyes against the spray. It was still dark, the raw edge of the January morning cutting into her exposed face and hands. Her crewmates – the older and experienced Tommy McCall on the helm, and young Callum, the village postman – were braced against the rough sea, their Sunday lie-in a distant memory.

The tasking request had come from Belfast Coastguard. A fishing boat, returning to Kirkcudbright, reported an Isle of Man-registered yacht, the *Ramsey Ranger*, dragging her anchor close to one of the Solway's treacherous sand-banks. The yacht's single crew member had refused the fishermen's help, so they'd relayed their concerns to the coastguard, who'd alerted the RNLI. The D-class *Margaret Wilson*, with her inflatable hull and shallow draught, was perfect for the job. It was a routine shout; they'd been out in worse.

'You were at the station fast,' Shona called to Tommy over the roar of the engine and constant buffeting of the wind. Sunday morning was training, but not until later. 'Has Freya kicked you out? Are you kipping next door in the boatyard?'

The relationship between Tommy and Freya was a recent development. Shona had welcomed the woman, who now worked at the village's Royal Arms pub, after they'd met on a complex historical murder case the year before.

'Less of your cheek, lady,' Tommy said, with a good-natured grin. 'I came down early to work on the *Silver Crest*. Got an enquiry fae a film crew wanting to hire her.' The old fishing boat was Tommy's pride and joy. 'Mibbaes I can put some B&B work your way at High Pines,' he told her. She recognised he was trying to cheer her up. January was always a lean month. She could really do with the business.

Callum, kneeling in the lifeboat's bow, spotted the target first. He indicated the direction with an outstretched arm and Tommy adjusted his course. The ten-metre yacht was listing badly, its mainsail flapping loose like an injured wing in the gloom. No sign of the yachtsman. Shona's heartbeat skipped up a notch at the possibility that this was now a *person in the water* shout, the RNLI's highest priority.

Tommy took them closer. Callum hailed to the vessel and switched on his torch. As the lifeboat was thrown about by the waves, the moving wedge of light revealed a reel of jagged images like an out-of-sync movie. The yacht's blue hull. The orange of the lifeboat. Angry frills of white water trailing like scratch marks across the shiny black of the sea.

A head appeared from the cabin doorway. The man, in his fifties, wore yellow wet-weather gear and a lifejacket, and had the deeply lined face of an experienced sailor. He peered at them, eyes screwed up against the light, then a hand shot out and shooed them away.

'Sir, I'd like to put a crew member aboard,' Tommy shouted.

The wind was blowing the yacht directly towards the Drumroof Bank on a falling tide. It would be impossible for the vessel to free herself from the sandbar without help.

The man glowered at Tommy, then shook his head and shrank back. 'I don't need your help. Keep away.'

Shona and Tommy exchanged a glance. It wasn't unusual for people to refuse assistance. Cold or dehydrated, they'd become confused. After sailing through the night, the single crew member on board was probably exhausted and not thinking straight.

'Let me have a word,' Shona said to Tommy. As a trained police negotiator, she had the experience. She shuffled forward on her knees, changing places with Callum in the bow of the lifeboat.

'Sir, my name's Shona,' she called. 'Are you injured?'

'Go away, I'm fine,' the man yelled, gripping the doorframe as the yacht corkscrewed in the swell.

'I just need to come aboard and check you're okay,' Shona said, with a reassuring smile. Callum's torch was still trained on the vessel. There was a smear of blood above the man's eye. A head injury might also explain his confusion. 'What's happened to your face? Can I take a quick look?'

'No! It's nothing. Leave me be.'

'Okay, sir,' Shona replied, calmly. Unlike many uncooperative individuals she'd faced in her beat days, she thought it was unlikely he'd take a swing at her if she got aboard, but in weather this rough she'd need his cooperation to make the transfer.

'What's your name, sir?' she persisted. 'Is there anyone expecting you? Your family? We can call them. Let them know you've been held up.'

He shook his head.

'Okay,' Shona said, concealing her thinning patience. 'Thing is, if you won't let me come over, just to confirm you're okay, I'll have to call in a coastguard patrol. They'll want to check your vessel over. Make sure it's fit to continue your journey.' She paused to let that thought sink in. Deal with me or deal with them. 'Less paperwork with the lifeboat.' She smiled.

The only way to save the yacht was to tow it from the sands into deeper water. Once aboard, she'd convince him. The waves were reflecting back off the emerging sandbar, creating a washing machine effect that, judging from the yachtsman's pallor, was taking its toll. Above, the sky had lightened a fraction, but instead of improving their situation, it merely revealed a menacing bank of cloud heading up the Solway from the Irish Sea. The yachtsman must have seen it too. His eyes darted between Tommy, the churning sea and Shona. A moment later, she saw his resolve falter.

'Okay. Just you, and only for a minute,' he said to Shona, touching the blood on his face with a shaking hand, as if he'd only just realised it was there.

Shona gave Tommy McCall the nod.

Fighting the swell, the helmsman had to time his approach between the ten-foot waves. She positioned herself on one knee, against the port side, hands gripping one of the lifeboat's black anchor points. A watery pit opened and closed between the two vessels. She was grateful that Callum's six-foot three inches of muscle was behind her, holding the straps of her lifejacket. He was also keeping an eye on the waves that advanced on the lifeboat like a ravenous pack of grey wolves.

'There's a big one coming,' Callum shouted.

Tommy moved quickly, closing on the yacht's starboard beam.

It was now or never.

Shona launched herself forward, planting a foot on the side of the lifeboat and grabbing for the yacht's guardrail. A second later she was over the lines, knees stinging as she hit the deck. Callum bundled the first-aid bag after her as the *Margaret Wilson* plummeted downwards and away. Shona felt a wave of relief that the solidity of the *Ramsey Ranger* was beneath her.

The yachtsman, who finally identified himself blearily as a Manxman by the name of Larry Smith, refused to move into the shelter of the cabin. Forced to assess him on the rolling deck, she established that his injuries consisted of nothing more than bruising, the blood coming from a minor graze above his eye. He was, however, clearly exhausted and showing signs of exposure. The depth gauge in the yacht's cockpit was flashing double zero, the pumps working at maximum and the anchor gone. The wind drove the stampeding waves before it, while the tide sucked the sea from beneath their feet. There was no time to do this gently.

'See that?' Shona pointed to the livid sky beyond the lifeboat. The storm had advanced on them with terrifying speed. When he nodded, she swung her arm towards Drumroof Bank, the sands emerging from the retreating waves like the back of some buried and hungry beast. 'Sandbank versus boat. Only gonna be one winner, Larry. Do you want to lose your vessel?'

This time he agreed to a tow.

Tommy turned the lifeboat, edging it near enough to get the line across. Shona helped to get the mainsail down, then went forward and sat with her legs dangling over each side of the *Ramsey Ranger*'s prow, inching as close to the pulpit rail as she could. The yacht bucked like a rodeo bull. Callum kneeled in the lifeboat, preparing to throw the towline.

'Breaking wave, breaking wave!'

Tommy's shout came just in time for Shona to see the two vessels lifted like a pair of toy ships. They careered towards each other, only to be yanked apart at the last minute. Callum let out a grunt of frustration as the tow line spun out to Shona but fell short, with a stinging splash of spray. He hauled it back and coiled it with practised speed.

He threw again and this time she grabbed the line, but as she went to make it fast, she saw a set of three big waves coming at her like a train. Though a weak sun had crossed the horizon, its faint light was submerged. It was hard to keep your bearings in this tumbling world of air and water. Callum's voice called out a warning somewhere close. Through the spray, Shona saw a wall of grey water approaching.

'Wave. Breaking wave!'

The second wave struck the yacht, spinning it ninety degrees and yanking the line from her hand. When she next saw the lifeboat, it was perched on top of the wave crest like a fairy on a Christmas tree, its navigation lights the only bright spots in the gloom. The water plunged again and by some miracle, the *Margaret Wilson* remained upright.

Tommy's first duty was to preserve not only the lifeboat but also her crew. They were reaching the limits within which they could safely operate. The sea drew back, bringing the vessels level once more. When Tommy

THE BAGPIPING PEOPLE

Selected Short Stories

Douglas Dunn

TURNPIKE BOOKS

ACKNOWLEDGEMENTS

The following stories first appeared in the *New Yorker*: 'The Bagpiping People', 'Bobby's Room', 'Boyfriends and Girlfriends', 'The Canoes', 'Fishermen', 'Orr Mount', 'Something for Little Robert' and 'South America'.

'More than Half the Way' first appeared in *London Magazine*.

This edition published by Turnpike Books 2017

turnpikebooks@gmail.com

ISBN 9780993591310

Typeset by RefineCatch Ltd, Bungay, Suffolk

Printed and bound in Great Britain by Clays Ltd, St Ives Plc

CONTENTS

SOUTH AMERICA

Thea Docherty left Glasgow for Barlochan in September of 1937. She rented a house on the outskirts of the village. With two children, and no husband in evidence, she was a subject of talk from the day she arrived.

'What age is she?'

'Young. In her twenties. Nice-looking woman.'

'And no man to be seen about the place? He must be in the Army, or at sea.'

'Maybe she's a widow.'

'Oh dear, don't say that, Mrs Barclay. Perhaps her husband's coming on later.'

'Leaving her to contend with a move? And to look after a pair of toddlers as well? No, her man's cleared out. That is, if she's married at all.'

Jack Docherty was a mining engineer, just beginning his career. A company with interests in Brazil recruited him in 1935. He talked about it with Thea, but Brazil seemed to her unlikely and exotic. She was unable to take it seriously. People like her never went to South America, and nothing would bring her to feel that Jack Docherty was any different.

'We're a wandering profession,' he said, announcing that he had accepted the offer. He was gently spoken, introspective, and self-assured. 'We have to think about the money,' he said. 'It's only for two years.' When that failed to satisfy her, he became angry – not loudly, but with a faint tremor in his voice that accused Thea of failing to encourage his ambition. 'Opportunities don't grow on trees! There's nothing interesting for me here in Scotland. Two years of good experience in Brazil will pave my way, Thea. Please, try to think of the future.'

Jack went to South America on his own. Early in 1937, he wrote from South America to say that his employers had offered to promote him to Senior Site Supervisor if he would agree to renew his contract for a further three years. Thea wrote back that she wanted him to come home. By May, Jack admitted that he intended to stay in Brazil at least until 1941.

'With one more promotion,' he wrote, in his formal but not unaffectionate manner, 'I shall be in a position to bring you and the children to Brazil, where we can live very well. This is a country of limitless opportunities for a man with knowledge and ability.'

Thea answered that she was sick of living in a tenement in Glasgow, sick of climbing stairs, sick of her neighbours, and sick of having to explain to people where he was and what he did. 'Janet was six weeks old when you left, and to all intents and purposes she's never seen you. Alistair says 'Daddy' to strangers in the street. He doesn't remember you. Come back to Scotland, Jack Docherty. Your family needs you.' She added that she was planning to find another place to live, near her family home.

Thea had been to Barlochan several times as a child, for she was brought up in Castle Stewart, a town a few miles away. Her father sent Thea information on suitable houses to rent in the district. She went home for a few days, and chose the Barlochan house.

'Don't you think it's a bit too big?' her father asked.

'It's cheap at the price,' she said. 'A Senior Site Supervisor can well afford it. I intend to be comfortable.'

Everyone knew everyone else in Barlochan, not just to look at or to talk to but by family history stretching as far back as handed-down memories can go. From snippets of information passed on by shopkeepers, or those who had spoken to her in the street, they soon knew a bit more about Thea Docherty.

'If her husband's in South America, then why's she in Barlochan?' one woman asked. 'I mean, Barlochan, of all places? They're the first new family in Barlochan in ten years.'

'She comes from Castle Stewart. Her maiden name's Masson. Her father has that shoe shop in Graham Street, down the road from the British Linen Bank.'

That Thea was nearly, if not precisely, local reassured the people of Barlochan. They could understand why a woman whose husband was overseas preferred to live closer to her parents. 'Why not in Castle Stewart itself, though, when her man's away like that?' the woman persisted, suspiciously. 'There's something wrong somewhere.'

Thea was friendly, and became popular. Local people approved of her dutiful and good-humoured propriety. She visited her parents and they visited her. Alistair and Janet were neat, clean, and well behaved.

'Off for a few days this time, Mrs Docherty?' asked Mr Crichton, the grocer, who stepped out of his shop when he saw Thea at the bus stop with luggage. Alistair, who was five and a half, stood on one side of her, and Janet, nearly four, held Thea's other hand.

'It seems a bit silly,' Thea said. 'Heading for Castle Stewart with two suitcases.'

'Mr and Mrs Masson keeping well?'

'Fine, thanks.'

'The postie showed me the Brazil stamps, so I know you had a letter from Mr Docherty the other day. It's amazing, isn't it, that a letter should come all that way and arrive safe and sound? Everything still all right out there?' the grocer asked.

'He loves his work,' Thea said.

Thea timed her visits to her parents to coincide with the arrival of her money from Jack at the Castle Stewart branch of the British Linen Bank. This time, though, Thea would stay for one night with her parents before leaving Alistair and Janet in their care and going up to Glasgow for a few days.

'Are you sure you're telling me the truth when you say you're going to visit a friend?' her mother asked – aware of Thea's husbandless days going by.

'Roberta Morrison's expecting me.' Thea saw that her mother considered herself deceived. 'Why would I lie to you, Mother?'

'There's bad feeling between you and Jack.' Mrs Masson sounded relieved that she had managed to say what had been bothering her for months. 'Don't deny it. It's nearly four years he's been there, wherever it is. Brazil,' she said, sounding the name as if it stood for failure. 'The man couldn't be content with nuts and coffee. He has to *go* there. Two years, that was his promise.' Her anger at Jack's faithless word seemed to be directed at Thea. 'It'll be six years by the time he gets back.'

'It's the money,' Thea said defensively. 'And it's his work, Mother. I wouldn't have married Jack if I hadn't known he'd a bit of get-up-and-go. He worked hard at night school. He's a mining engineer. He's trying to make a better life for us.'

'I hope it's worth it,' Mrs Masson said, bitterly. 'All that loneliness for you and hard work for him.'

'Don't think I don't miss him,' Thea said, 'because I do. But I've got to have some kind of a life, Mother, even if it's no more than a visit to a friend like Roberta once in a while. She's been down to stay with me and the children at Barlochan whenever she could, and she's been asking me for ages to go and see her.'

Thea had met her schoolteacher friend at a French class in Glasgow years back – before Alistair was born. Roberta was red-haired, vivacious, rather plain, and still unmarried; she was devoted to teaching children and to attending evening courses.

'Why are you brushing up your French if you don't ever want to go to France?' Thea had asked.

'I wouldn't have the nerve,' Roberta answered. 'I've started Italian, too. And don't ask me – I've no intention of going to Italy, either. You know what Italians are like – worse even than Frenchmen. Or so I've read.'

In Roberta's favour were the politely animated soirées she threw once or twice a year. Most of her male friends were ex-classmates from university or the teacher-training college, and most of them were spoken for. Those who were unattached seemed to have decided that Roberta was a good sort but definitely not their type.

'It feels like a hundred years since I was at one of Roberta's parties,' Thea complained to her mother.

'Does Jack know these people?'

'Yes, he used to go with me. I'm dying for some decent conversation.'

'It doesn't sound like Jack's sort of company,' her mother said.

Thea knew she was lying to herself – that she was going to Glasgow for more than Roberta's company. She blamed Jack for the enticements of a betrayal she did not want to commit. She resented having been made to feel unnecessarily sour. Almost four years without Jack had given her more than an unwanted independence. Each additional month of separation made clearer the sense that she had been neglected and deserted. It worsened until it became an inner rancour that she tired of disguising by small talk exchanged on the streets of Barlochan, or by pretending to her mother that Jack's ambition was more admirable than selfish. The thought of Jack tinkering contentedly with machines in Brazil maddened her. She pictured him supervising workmen in the mine, in a landscape she could not imagine, or spending his evenings poring over geological data and in technical conversations with other absent husbands.

War was a month off when Thea decided she had no choice but to tell her mother she was pregnant.

Mrs Masson said nothing at first but continued with the washing-up until it seemed she could no longer bear the noise of the crockery in the basin. Drying her hands, she said tartly, 'Who's the father? Roberta Morrison?'

Mr Masson was outside talking to a neighbour at the foot of the garden beside the compost heap. 'I don't have the heart to tell him,' Mrs Masson said. 'You can't stay in Barlochan. It's a small place. They'll make your life a misery. Do you know what you've done?' Mrs Masson was angry and puzzled, indignant that no appropriate emotion showed on her daughter's face. 'You might at least apologize to me, no matter what you're planning to tell Jack. Why? I never took you to be so stupid as to – So why?'

'I wanted another baby,' Thea said.

Thea wrote to Roberta Morrison: 'Come down if you can. It'll be your winter holidays. You can hold my hand. I don't know whether to laugh or cry, but I'll make my mind up when the baby's born.' Staggered by the news, Roberta choked on her scandalized decency and on Thea's jaunty style. But she heeded her friend's call and went to Barlochan, where Ivor was delivered by the local midwife in Thea's house. The war was four months old.

'You'd think one more baby in the world wouldn't make much difference,' the midwife said to Roberta, 'but there'll be blue murder when Mr Docherty gets back. I know Mrs Docherty's father.' Mrs MacBain held out a foot and pointed to a sensible shoe. 'I bought these in his shop. She told me she just wanted another baby. Did she tell you the same?'

'Whatever she wanted,' Roberta said, 'we know what she's got.'

'What'll I say to Mr Masson the next time I need to buy a pair of shoes? 'How's wee Ivor?' The man's face'll drop at my feet. Well, I'll away and break the news to gossips worse than me. Dr Geddes'll come and see them in the morning.'

Roberta stayed for two weeks. 'I wish you'd think about moving, Thea. I feel their eyes on me when I go down the street here. 'How's Mrs Docherty?' 'Mother and baby doing fine? Oh, that's good.' It's not what they say; it's the way they say it. They make me feel like I've done something terrible. It must be worse for you.'

'If I could put up with it while I was carrying the baby,' Thea said, 'I can put up with it now he's been born. They won't forget, but they'll get used to it. They aren't such bad people.'

'How can you be so charitable when you know perfectly well how they talk behind your back?'

'I like it here,' Thea said decisively, 'and I see no reason to leave.'

'What about Jack? What about the war?'

'Will you shut up about the war? I'm sick of it!'

'It might prevent Jack from getting home,' Roberta said. 'Even if it doesn't – Well, I suppose it doesn't matter now. It's all over between you and him, that's for sure.'

'I don't see why,' Thea said.

'Thea! How can you write and *not* tell him?'

'I need the money he sends,' Thea snapped.

'Are you serious?' It had been a strenuous few days for Roberta. She was unused to childbirth, in any circumstances. She thought of Thea as her closest friend – long-suffering, indomitable Thea, who had given up on patience and allowed Jack's absence to change her. 'I never thought I'd hear you say that.'

'You're feeling guilty,' Thea said, 'because you introduced me to Ivor's father. I'm sorry. I shouldn't have reminded you.'

'I imagine he'll join the forces,' Roberta said, speculating romantically on the disappearance of Thea's lover into the vastness of life and time.

'He's just the type,' Thea said sardonically.

'Do you know him well enough to be able to say that?' Roberta said, defending the father of Thea's child.

'He struck me as a decent sort. Don't you feel bad about him? Thea, you involved a perfectly decent, nice man in the ruin of your marriage.'

'He's as decent as I am,' Thea said. 'I don't blame you if you object to having to keep a secret. But if anyone's to blame because I got lonely enough to find someone else, then it's Jack Docherty – Jack who isn't here, Jack who's been in Brazil for four and a half years. I've life left in me yet and I intend to live it, Jack or no Jack.'

'But I thought you still loved him,' Roberta said, helplessly. 'Don't you – in spite of everything?'

'I do,' Thea said, surprised that she should be questioned. She lifted the baby from its cot and unbuttoned her blouse. 'I do,' she said.

Women in Barlochan suspected that Ivor's father might be a local man. Thea was confronted by their qualms as she waited for Alistair outside the school gates in the huddle of mothers whose children had no older brothers or sisters to escort them home.

'Take it from me, ladies, I don't make dirt in my own midden. I go away to do things like that. All right? So the next time you see me at the bus stop with a suitcase,' Thea said, casually defiant, 'you'll know I'm off on the razzle-dazzle. I probably won't be, but you'll say I am.'

'Mr Docherty due home soon from South America?' Mrs Munro's voice rode impishly on her question.

'I'm afraid not,' Thea said. 'Mr Docherty will be down the foreign mines for some time yet, chipping rocks with a wee hammer, no doubt.'

'I'm dying to ask you,' Mrs Gillespie said, rubbing her hands. 'Do you think you'll get away with it?'

'God forbid that babies should ever be against the law!' Thea said laughingly, and the women laughed with her.

'I was meaning when your man gets back,' Mrs Gillespie said seriously.

'If I were to let you in on my secret, you'd tell everyone else, Mrs Gillespie, and then you'd all be at it. Society round here would go to pot! No, I couldn't live with the responsibility.'

She knew she had given them something to laugh at. There were no broken marriages in Barlochan, although these women were familiar with marriages made elsewhere than in Heaven, some of them their own. They looked at Thea, wondering if she was stupid or very brave. She knew she had also given them a chance to say behind her back, 'She'll laugh on the other side of her face when her man gets home, when he steps off that bus and sees her pushing a pram.'

Letters from Jack took longer to reach Barlochan now, and came at irregular intervals. A few arrived stamped 'Delayed by Enemy Action'. Sometimes her replies included snapshots of herself, Alistair, and Janet. She gave him news of their progress. She mentioned all the local characters without mentioning that she had become one herself. Each time she wrote to Jack, she went once again over the question of whether to tell him about Ivor. In imaginary conversations with him, she explained her simple motive: 'I wanted another baby and you weren't here.' She accused him of selfishness. 'What do you expect if you stay away for six years? I used to say to myself, Jack Docherty, that if you'd any family or friends you wouldn't have stayed away from me all that time. You'd have had more to call your home. But that doesn't say much for me, does it? How do you think I feel when I read out your messages to Alistair and Janet: 'Be a good child and do well at school and look after Mummy for me'? I don't feel proud, Jack.'

Thea's misgivings demanded that she keep Jack in ignorance for as long as she could. The family could never do without the monthly payments he sent.

'There's war work in Greenock,' Thea remarked to her parents. 'They're looking for women to train as machinists.'

'You?' her father said. 'A machinist for the war effort? And Greenock's miles away!'

'I don't give a damn for the war effort,' Thea said. 'I need something to do.'

'What about the children?' her mother asked. 'Ivor's too young to be left with us.'

'You're right,' Thea said. 'God forbid that I should do a Jack Docherty on them. It just crossed my mind.'

'If you're needing a change,' her father said, 'why don't you go up to Glasgow and see Roberta?'

'If I did that,' Thea said, 'Mother would think I was off on a fertility spree.'

Mrs Masson thought about it. 'I can trust you not to be daft twice,' she said.

When Thea got home to Barlochan that day, there was a letter from Jack saying that he would be staying on in Brazil until the war ended. She read and reread the letter for suitable signs of sorrow or regret, but gave it up as a waste of time. Jack described at length the responsibilities of his new position as Regional Engineer. Thea went to Glasgow with one purpose in mind.

'A man, a big-hearted man, might forgive or get used to one spare bairn about the house. But two – no, no, two's enough for a man not to feel safe,' Mr Masson said, between groans of worn fortitude. 'I used to think you were the most sensible girl I ever met. That last time, I took a blow. I really did. And now this.

You're not even upset! Same as last time – not so much as a tear in your eye.' He was puzzled by Thea's composure. 'You should be ashamed, but you aren't. You ought to be scared stiff, but I don't see any signs of that, either.'

'Why should I be ashamed? I wanted another baby, and I'm going to have one. Did I ask Jack to go to South America?'

Her father waved at her to stop. 'You'll have to write and tell him,' he said. 'It isn't honest to leave a man in such terrible ignorance.'

'You mean he deserves to know. All right, I'll tell him,' Thea said. 'As soon as I've given birth.'

'Thea,' Mr Masson pleaded, 'go and console your mother. Behave to her as a daughter should in your position. Give her at least one hint of shame or remorse for her to hold on to.'

Edward was born in April 1943. Mrs MacBain brought Dr Geddes with her, but the midwife's hunch that the birth might be difficult proved wrong. Dr Geddes had nothing to do but urge Thea to push, while Mrs MacBain shouted back at him, 'What do you know about it?'

Thea was half asleep with exhaustion and relief when she was awakened by the sound of Dr Geddes's voice talking to Roberta and Mrs MacBain in the next room. 'It's a load off our minds that there aren't too many servicemen stationed round here. Otherwise, Mrs MacBain and I would be bringing more little strangers into the world with fathers not properly accounted for.'

'We had one a fortnight ago,' Mrs MacBain said, nudging Dr Geddes's memory. 'Mrs Archibald, two years wed, and her man in the Navy. He was away less than a year – eleven months and a week, for I added it up – and then his wife drops a daughter.'

'Old Mr Archibald came in to see me,' the doctor said. 'He was wondering if there was such a biological fluke as an eleven months' gestation. Eighteen months in elephants, I told him, nine in the human female.'

'What was that?' Thea shouted from the bedroom. 'Mrs MacBain! Who's that you're talking about?'

'You should be resting,' Mrs MacBain chided.

'Did I hear you say that Sheila Archibald gave birth?' Thea asked, pugnacious with happy surprise.

'You'd have heard it sooner or later,' Dr Geddes said, 'but don't tell anyone you heard it from me. Her folks are trying to hush it up.'

'I wondered why I hadn't seen her. The slut!' Thea said with satisfaction. 'And her man in peril on the high seas. He'd hardly turned his back on her – disgusting!' She laughed.

'Oh, Thea, how can you be so cock-a-hoop at a time like this?' Roberta said, appealing to Dr Geddes and Mrs MacBain to support her low opinion of yet another scandal.

'Now, now,' said Dr Geddes, 'we mustn't distress Mrs Docherty. You must be very tired,' he said to Thea. 'You should be resting.'

'Tired my foot! I'm jubilant! Poor, loyal Roberta. I don't think you'll ever understand me,' Thea said. 'I'm proud. I'm really proud of this one,' she said, kissing her new baby. 'You'll have a wee friend,' she told him. 'Someone just like you.'

Thea stood on the step before the teller's elevated wooden counter in the British Linen Bank. 'The manager would like a word with you, Mrs Docherty.' The teller pointed to the glassed-in office.

'I'm sorry, but these monthly drafts have been curtailed,' the manager said.

'Is it the war?' Thea asked. She was frightened, but she had known it was only a matter of time before she had this interview with the bank manager.

'It could be a new currency regulation introduced by the Brazilian banks. Wartime does that,' he said. 'I've written to Glasgow to find out.' He looked at a document in the file before him. 'So far, my instructions are that Mr Docherty's standing order in your favour is now in abeyance. We should receive clarification in a few days.'

'Does it say 'until further notice'?' Thea asked.

'No. Can you think of a reason why it might be cancelled?'

'I can think of a couple of excuses,' Thea said, 'but I can't think of a reason. Can you recommend a good lawyer?' She wondered if she was serious, and decided that she was.

She had half expected it since she wrote to Jack introducing the existence of Ivor and Edward. Still, his indirect but practical answer was a shock.

'I know that in the eyes of everyone except me I've wronged Jack Docherty,' she told the lawyer, Mr Birnley. 'But he started it. He wronged me first by going to South America. All right, I accepted two years, even with two children to bring up. I indulged his career. And eight years have passed! South America!' she shouted. 'What sort of place is that to be when his wife's here, and Germans and God knows who else could've been baying at my door? I feel his wrong to me day by day and week by week.'

'And yet it's no fault of Mr Docherty's that you now have four children to bring up.'

'I've been trying to explain just that!' Thea said.

Birnley was intrigued by her combativeness. He was familiar with the human habit of taking the offensive to excuse one's criminal or immoral act, but he could not recall coming across a woman who asserted devious justifications with such barefaced poise. It was his experience that women clients were often timid. Imminent litigation and its formal authority awed them; their tongues were humbled by proximity to the great institutions of respectability and truth. Their limited vocabularies stuttered into attempts to prove that they were good at heart. Guilty or not guilty, they usually wept, but he felt you could always see when a woman was telling the truth. Thea's rugged aplomb amused him, as did the challenge she posed to his skills.

'The news about little – ah, Ivor,' he said. 'Well, news of that sort, coming straight out of the blue – I mean, Mr Docherty might not want to . . .' Whatever he meant to say vanished in gestures. 'You may be asking too much of him if you expect him to understand, to forgive, your moral or instinctive lapse . . . your little error, Mrs Docherty. Two little errors, Mrs Docherty, two – yes, to be candid, two contraventions of your marriage vows. Why didn't you write to him sooner?'

'I didn't see any point in worrying the man unnecessarily,' she said. 'It's not easy to explain a thing like that in a letter. You think about it. And what's this about lapses? Errors? I never did anything I didn't intend to! I might be all too human, but I'm not a fool.'

'I find myself quite able to understand your husband's feelings,' Mr Birnley said, leaning across his desk and using his sternest gaze to probe Thea's character.

'Feelings be damned! It's a thoughtless husband who'd stay in Brazil for as long as he has and then cut us off without a penny. Two of the children *are* his, in case you've forgotten.' She looked at the lawyer with grave determination – so closely that he had to turn away. 'Are you trying to wriggle out of a case you don't know how to turn down?' she demanded. 'Are you trying to work out whether you can afford it? All I'm asking is that you write to him and point out the dire consequences poverty might have on his children, Alistair and Janet. Take a note of their names. I'll fend for the other two.' Her tone challenging, she said, 'Don't imagine that I'm irresponsible.'

'That's reasonable enough,' Mr Birnley said, without conviction.

'Too reasonable!' Thea said. 'I've compromised.'

'A fair man recognizes reason when he sees it,' the lawyer said.

'Oh, is that a fact?' Thea said ironically. 'And tell Jack Docherty I'm willing to have him back, in spite of what he's made me do.'

'You want Mr Docherty – You want *me* to ask Mr Docherty to come *back* to you?' the lawyer asked slowly, dwelling on his bewildered emphases.

'I want to live in a house with a man in it,' Thea said. 'My man. I made my bed, and I'll lie in it, given half a chance.'

Six months went by and there was no answer to the lawyer's letter. 'He may not want to reply,' Mr Birnley suggested. 'There's also the uncertainty of the wartime mails. Ships are sent to the bottom and planes are shot out of the sky. These are daily occurrences, Mrs Docherty. For all we know, there may be an embargo on your husband's leaving Brazil, especially to attend to – not unimportant business, I grant you, but personal. Mining is an essential industry. Ores,' he said, speaking to Thea's simmering impatience, 'make metals, which go into ships, guns, tanks, planes. Your husband may well be considered indispensable.'

'Don't talk to me about ores! I know more about ores than you do.'

Barlochan noticed that Thea Docherty had less money to spend. She sometimes asked the grocer for credit. Women had often remarked that Thea's children were the best turned out in the village; their reputation for perfection began to dwindle. Mr Masson gave Thea money, but not much, or often enough, and she was too proud to ask for more. She wrote to the welfare department in the government offices at Castle Stewart. Someone was sent to see her.

'Your house seems a little on the large side,' said the official, a middle-aged woman whose eyes roved professionally around Thea's living room. 'Couldn't you find something smaller, less expensive to run?'

'I've four children,' Thea said.

Thea told her how Jack had gone to South America in 1935, and of the punctual monthly payments that had stopped almost a year before.

'Nineteen thirty-five?' the official asked, her eyes weighing up the room as she underlined that date in her notebook. 'Ivor's such a lovely, unusual name,' the woman said to Thea. 'I seldom come across it. I take it that Mr Docherty's at least managed to get over on leave a couple of times?'

'Unfortunately,' Thea said, 'Mr Docherty's been too deeply involved in the South American economy.'

'I see,' said the official. 'Then that's almost nine years he's been away?'

'He was very, very good at writing to me,' Thea said, slyly.

'I can see that a rather remarkable correspondence has been taking place; I can see that for myself.' The woman closed her notebook with a decisive slam. It sounded like a door closing. 'Frankly, I don't believe there's all that much we can do for you, Mrs Docherty. Money's awfully tight, and there are so many cases of hardship at the moment. The best I can promise you is that your case will come before the board in due course. We'll let you know.' She stood up. 'Personally, I feel that a smaller house would make a big difference to your circumstances.'

'You're standing there thinking I've got myself into a right mess, aren't you?' Thea said aggressively.

'It's not for me to judge. I see so many different cases. It's water off a duck's back to me.'

'But you *are* judging.'

'Only in the sense that I doubt if my department would take this case very far. You have quite some way to go before you would qualify as a charge on what little funds we have for poor relief.'

'You look as if you're eating something delicious, and far too good for the likes of me,' Thea said. 'No, I'll drop it altogether. I'm sorry I bothered you.'

Thea went to work in her father's shoe shop, taking Ivor and Edward with her each day to Castle Stewart and bringing them back on the evening bus. 'I'll do anything,' she said, 'but I won't give up my house, Jack Docherty or no Jack Docherty.'

Roberta came down as often as she could, and one November day she and Thea took the children to the coast, a few miles away. They walked along the beach as the wild, grey wind swept in over the sea. 'You're a teacher, Roberta,' Thea said. 'You should know. Which way is South America?'

'That way,' Roberta said, after a hesitant pointing that stopped when she felt she had the direction right. 'Really, I don't know. I think it's that way.' Thea looked along the line of Roberta's arm. 'Ireland's blocking your view!' Roberta shouted as Thea took Edward from his pram and walked closer to the sea. 'You aren't looking straight at South America!'

'Ireland be damned!' Thea said. 'Alistair! Janet!' she shouted. 'Come and look at South America!'

There was no news of Jack until the war was over by almost a year. Mr Birnley called Thea into his office to show her a letter he had received from a solicitor in London. It said that Mr Docherty, of the Southern Hemisphere Mining Corporation, no longer wished to communicate with his wife, and that in view of her repeated infidelities he felt under no obligation to contribute to her financial support.

Mr Birnley made clicking noises with his tongue, waiting for time to pass. He pulled a handkerchief from his pocket and blew his nose, his eyes fixed on Thea as she studied the solicitor's letter. 'He's being very harsh,' he said. 'I expected the offer of a sum for Alistair and Janet. We'll pursue it, of course.'

'No, don't,' Thea said, still rereading.

'We'd be better placed to demand provision for Alistair and Janet if you were to commence divorce proceedings,' Mr Birnley said. 'I doubt if the court would sympathize with your attitude to two additional children born out of marriage,' he said. 'But Mr Docherty's prolonged sojourn in Brazil can be considered in two phases. First from 1935 to the conception of little Ivor, and the second after that event. Please, don't interrupt me,' he said, his hand waving to hush Thea's protestations. 'I know your views on this subject. But I must advise you of the best legal tactic. That first stage of absence was a long one, involving a broken promise to you. There's a case there. His obsession with his career in South America contributed greatly to the wreck of a marriage which a little consideration for you could easily have saved. I can hear a first-rate lawyer make an excellent argument out of that.' He looked pleased. 'What do you think?'

'I think he's still in South America,' Thea said.

Thea wrote to Brazil and told Jack that she had no intention of initiating a divorce, and that if he took the first step she would fight it until everyone believed that his selfishness was to blame for all that had happened. There was no answer. She wrote again: 'You can come home now, you stupid man. If it's your pride that's been bothering you, surely to God there's been enough time for your wounds to have healed.' It was like talking to the night sky.

'You should stop believing that Jack'll come home, walk through that door, and forgive you,' Roberta said in 1950. She was visiting Barlochan again, this time to interview for a post in the local primary school. 'He's been gone for fifteen years! Are you sure you'd recognize him? How could you live together after all that's happened?'

'I don't even like him,' Thea said. 'Roberta, you've loved my children and you've brooded over me. You've been a great help, a lovely friend, and I'll always be grateful. But you still think I've got what I deserve, don't you?' Her tone was quiet but exasperated and disappointed. 'You think that I was reckless and impatient, that I didn't 'wait' for Jack. Well, I did and I didn't. More did than didn't, in my opinion. If you're going to come to live here, I ought to know what you really think of me.'

'I haven't got the job yet,' Roberta said.

'And being Thea Docherty's friend won't be the best recommendation in Barlochan.'

'I don't know about that,' Roberta said. 'I'm not sure what I think about you, and, if you ask me, the people round here don't know what to think, either. But I've spent a lot of time here, and now and then I get the feeling that they actually admire you. I suppose I do, too. After all, I haven't had a very exciting life. So far,' she said, touching wood. 'The best part of it may have been your . . . well, I don't know what to call them.'

'Mistakes?'

'As a candidate for the post of headmistress of Barlochan Primary, I ought to call them mistakes, or worse. But no – I wouldn't let anyone call Ivor and Edward 'mistakes'.'

At her interview the next day, the school panel, which included Dr Geddes among other local worthies, questioned Roberta at length on her views on primary education, and seemed pleased with her answers.

'Excellent references,' the chairman said, leafing again through her file.

'Thank you,' said Roberta.

'We understand you have connections in Barlochan,' he went on.

'Yes,' she replied. 'An old friend, Mrs Thea Docherty.' She looked at Dr Geddes, who smiled at her. She took a deep breath. 'I ought to say that if I get the position I'll be moving in with her on a permanent basis. Her house is large, even with four children, and we've been friends for a very long time.' She felt herself to have been challenging and strong, perhaps for the first time in her life. But her spirited declaration didn't so much as raise an eyebrow. It was all water under the bridge.

'Thank you, then. We have two other candidates to interview, and we hope to reach a decision tomorrow morning. Will you be at Mrs Docherty's?'

'Yes,' said Roberta.

Dr Geddes winked at her, and gallantly escorted her to the door.

'Ah,' said a panel member. 'I see you've done extensive study in Italian language and literature. I work with a committee for the repair of war damages in Pisa.' He leaned to look at a fellow-Italophile on the panel.

Roberta was embarrassed to speak from the door. 'I'm afraid I've never been to Italy,' she said. 'The war . . .'

'One day you really must – particularly with your interest in Italian. Well, it's been a pleasure.'

Dr Geddes winked again, and closed the door behind her.

'So much for local scandal,' she said to Thea the next day, when she was offered the job. 'I'm surprised – stunned. They must have been able to tell just by the look of me that Barlochan Primary's in no danger of exposure to moral turpitude.'

'Aunt Roberta, did you ever meet my father?' Alistair asked one day.

'Yes, long ago. Several times. The last time I saw him, Janet had just been born.'

'If you want to know about your father,' said Thea angrily as she entered the room, 'then you ask *me*.'

'I have asked you.'

'And I've told you. The sooner we forget that scoundrel the better.'

'Then why did you write to him at Christmas?' Alistair said. 'I saw the envelope before you posted it. In Castle Stewart,' he told Roberta, 'so the Barlochan postie wouldn't know her business.'

'Thea!' Roberta said. 'Did you?'

'Well, it was Christmas,' Thea protested quietly. 'I sent him a Christmas card.'

THE BAGPIPING PEOPLE

Two or three mornings a week, in summer, a tinker called Robertson bagpiped the Gilchrist family from sleep half an hour before the time set on its alarm clocks. He played on the hoof, walking along the edge of a narrow plantation of birch trees.

'I thought you liked bagpipes,' said Jim Gilchrist, teasing his father's short temper at the breakfast table. 'Any time there's a pipe band on the wireless, you always have it turned up. You're the man who wants to go to the Edinburgh Tattoo. Military nostalgia,' he said, with a lighthearted, sneering conclusiveness. 'It's like a plague in this country. I don't suppose you noticed, but last winter there seemed more pipe bands on the wireless than usual. Suez.'

'Is that a fact?' Mr Gilchrist replied.

'No different,' said Jim, 'from these countries you read about where the radio stations pump out military music while the rebels and the government troops fight it out on the streets. Hungary,' he said, the way he had said 'Suez' a moment before.

'I worry about your mind,' said his father, before tasting his first spoonful of porridge. 'Aw, Sadie! You haven't salted it! Again,' he said wearily, plopping his spoon into his plate.

'I did salt it,' his wife said, with her back to them as she turned the frying bacon and eggs with a fish server. Almost to herself, she added, 'I salted it the same as I always salt it.'

Sam Gilchrist's porridge never seemed salty enough on these mornings when Robertson's piping woke him up at six. While he sprinkled extra salt on his porridge, his son measured a spoonful of sugar and then, when he knew his father was watching him, sifted it over his porridge.

'Men,' Mr Gilchrist said, with a jab of his spoon, 'don't put sugar on their porridge.'

'I don't see why not,' Jim said. 'You put jam on your cheese.'

'When the tinker's pipes make him so bad-tempered,' Mrs Gilchrist said, 'you'd think he'd take the trouble to ask the man to play half an hour later, when he's up anyway. Would that be unreasonable?'

'Perfectly reasonable,' said Jim.

His father left the table and opened both kitchen windows. Robertson's piping was too far away to be loud, but there was no doubting it was there.

'They're tinkers,' said Sadie Gilchrist. 'They're used to taking a telling. Used to it,' she emphasized, 'week in, week out. It's not as if your father would be asking him never to play within our hearing. Half an hour. What's half an hour in a busy day?'

'I don't mind when or where he plays,' said Gilchrist.

'He says he doesn't mind.' She sighed with disbelief. 'You minded, loudly, at six this morning! He says he doesn't mind! You should've heard him.'

The Robertsons and other tinker families lived in an untidy encampment two fields away from the Gilchrists' house. Tarpaulins were stretched over arched metal supports to form tents. It looked like a village of nomadic tribesmen. They possessed a small, open-backed lorry, three horse-drawn carts, and a number of ponies that grazed on lane-side grass or in the waste ground between the pillboxes and blast walls of a wartime anti-aircraft gun position.

By nine in the morning, Robertson would take up his station on the tree-darkened minor road that descended to the ferry. All day in summer, he piped up and down the queues of waiting cars. At times, the queues were long and profitable. In bad weather, only a few cars waited in a short, wet line of mechanized patience. Commercial vehicles, whose drivers were working and not on the road for pleasure, gave no money and were a waste of the piper's wind and skill. Robertson wore a kilt, brown jacket, and off-white open-necked shirt, and went sockless in a pair of brown brogues blanched by a lack of polish and too much weather and walking. He was followed by his daughter. She was about seventeen, and she wore the same green dress day after day, and the same patched sweater. The only variation in her clothing was a light scarf she tied under her chin. Red-haired, flushed, sullen, and barefooted for effect, she had the job of rattling the change in her cloth moneybag at the windows of each car. When it rained, father and daughter stood together under the overhang of the trees – never in the wooden shelter for pedestrians and cyclists.

To contend with the summer traffic, the ferry employed an extra hand, and for the last three years this summer job had been Jim Gilchrist's. At each end of the dismal vessel was a metal ramp, raised and lowered on chains, which when dropped on the cobbled gradients that led into the water allowed the vehicles to drive on and off. Superstructure on either side of the craft rose to an upper deck with benches that doubled as life rafts. On fine days most passengers went up on deck. In the middle of the ferry there was room for ten cars, fewer if a bus or a lorry or a furniture removal van got there first. Entire cycling clubs, local pedestrians, ramblers, hitch-hikers all used the ferry, as well as holidaying motorists, and vans and lorries on every conceivable commercial mission. People came from miles around to watch the ferry's clumsy, clanking, humorous crossings, to wonder at its workhorse appearance, its homely, functional looks, its strength, and then to take a round trip.

Ice cream could be bought from Italian vans on either side of the river. Small boys used the ferry for imaginary adventures. The river stank of oil and an unmistakable, non-specific industrial aroma compounded of shipbuilding, engineering, and the city of Glasgow, through which it flowed before reaching there. Often, the ferry waited for freighters to go by. Passengers waved to sailors, and the ships hooted as their wash approached the ferry and waves broke on the cobbled spits, sluicing around the wheels of the cars as they boarded slowly and carefully, and a ferryman ushered them to come on faster.

Ashton, one of the regular conductors, spent much of his time chasing after passengers and asking to see their tickets. He lived in the hope of catching locals from the south bank whom Jim had let on board free of charge. Jim watched Ashton double-checking tickets, and in his turn he kept his eyes open for natives of the north bank whom Ashton's counter-generosity allowed to cross without paying the fare.

'That was my brother you charged, Jim,' Ashton said.

'Sorry, Wattie. I'd no idea.'

'No idea? He crosses this river twice a day! He even looks like me. If you think you can come it wi' me, then forget it. It's no skin off my nose if your father knows a big wheel in the Navigational Trust,' he said, prodding Jim in the chest. 'I'm a lifelong socialist. I don't hold wi' this job-getting through friends of friends or who your daddy knows.'

'So what? I'm a lifelong socialist myself.'

'You? You aren't even weaned yet.'

The ferry was pulled across on parallel chains turned on board in engine houses that were open for small boys and their fathers to watch. 'Lovely piece of engineering!' 'You're doing a fine job there!' men called to the engineer, who felt himself to be the most watched man in Scotland. Each time the vessel left its cobbled, slippery jetties and the tension was taken up on the chains, they whipped out of the water with a dripping shudder. Women hid their faces in their hands with fear that the massive links might snap, and the strange blue-and-white metal box in which they were crossing the river end up drifting at the mercy of the current as helplessly as a biscuit tin.

'Stand back from the chains there!' Ashton's manner had the fulsome pomposity of the ancient trade of ferryman.

'If you had your way, Ashton, you'd ban bridges. Your days are numbered. One day, the twentieth century'll get wise to this contraption.'

When he wasn't playing his pipes and Jim walked past, the tinker always had a civil greeting. 'And how's the wee boatie?'

Like everyone else, Jim brought sandwiches for lunch, but he was the only one who went ashore to eat them. Jim never saw Robertson or his daughter eat anything. They went over the wall up the road from the ferry ramp, and into the park that surrounded a hospital for disabled and blind ex-servicemen. There they lit a fire in the same spot every day, seven days a week, and brewed tea.

'That's a very old-looking set of pipes you play, Mr Robertson.' Jim imagined that the girl looked surly because she didn't like his knowing their name. It was known among their own kin and kind, but apart from that it was known only to inquisitive policemen, various inspectors from the County Council, and a few farmers. 'How old are they?' Jim asked.

'What would a summer boatie like you know about pipes and pibroch?' said Robertson as he stooped over his fire.

'Nothing,' Jim admitted.

'And you don't look as if you want to learn,' the tinker said slyly, smiling over his tin mug of tea. 'Auld pipes,' he said, 'play auld tunes.'

'I'm one of the few people in this world who hear them at six in the morning,' Jim said amiably.

'You've heard me play,' said Robertson, 'you've heard the best you'll ever hear.'

'Would you like a sandwich?' Jim asked father and daughter. 'I've got more than I need. My mother thinks there must be two of me.' The girl nodded a surprised no and walked away, scattering the dregs of her tea on the ground. Strong tea brewed on an open fire and drunk from tin mugs clutched in hot hands is not to be despised, and Jim hoped that Robertson would offer him some. 'I've egg, salmon paste, or dried dates,' he told the tinker.

'No palm trees where I come from,' said Robertson. He took another drink of tea, with an audible slurp.

'I don't suppose my father's complained to you about your six-in-the-morning rehearsals?'

'Your dad and me get on right fine,' said Robertson.

'But you play all day, every day. It must be some strain on the wind. I don't understand why you'd want to play at six in the morning as well.'

'The last time I saw your dad, he was telling me how he fair misses it when I'm gone. He gave me a dozen eggs that time, and he promised to have a word wi' the farmer, Irvine, and pave the way for my two boys, helping them to a paid job for a week or two. Which your father did. He's a man whose word's as good as a deed done. They'll no' find it easy to make that man change as the clock changes, for all his prosperity.'

Summer was Sam Gilchrist's busiest time of the year. He ran a garage, and the major part of his business lay in the sale and repair of tractors and other agricultural machinery. He was beginning to prosper with the nineteen-fifties and saw better times ahead. He worked hard, and it was after seven by the time he got home. He ate, smoked, read the newspaper, dozed with it on his lap; then he woke up and stretched, yawned, and said, 'Right. Bedtime.'

'Your father,' said Sadie Gilchrist, 'is a wonderful conversationalist.'

'I hear you gave the tinker a dozen eggs,' Jim said. 'This is a man who gives handouts to an alarm clock.'

'And you're the man who's over-fond of his bed. Pass them a few eggs now and then,' said Gilchrist, 'and they'll be less inclined to help themselves. I've known men like Robertson go through a hen hut just like that – *psst*,' he said, cutting his throat with his forefinger. 'And there's your eggs gone, and half your hens as well.'

'And then he uses his influence with Sandy Irvine. Jobs,' said Jim, 'for two tinkers. He's even told Robertson how much he dotes on his bagpiping.'

'Don't complain, then,' said Sadie Gilchrist, 'if he serenades us outside the bedroom window.'

'I go a long way back with Robertson. It's not how I'd live, but he has a decent streak, and it suits me to give him a helping hand when I feel like it.'

During his lunch-hours, Jim observed the habits of the motorists as Robertson piped and his daughter begged with her jangling moneybag. He saw men and women open their car doors and listen with folklorist attentiveness. In his ferryman's uniform, he felt like a cross between a naval officer and a bus conductor; he noticed them size him up as an object of curiosity. Many people gave the girl a copper coin or two with a smile and good grace. Others wound up their windows and looked away when it came their turn for the tinker's daughter to shake her cloth bag before them. Her look then was sharp and peremptory. Jim saw people begin conversations with their companions when they saw her coming, to give the impression that they were too busy doing something else to notice she was there.

At the busiest times, the queue, the ferry, the riverside had the atmosphere of a fair. Children ran down the line of cars to and from the ice cream vans. Money changed hands for ice cream, lemonade, and bagpiping. The Hospital for Disabled Ex-Servicemen had a small showroom at its park gate in which the patients displayed and sold their wares in basketwork. Coin boxes for donations towards the hospital's work were carried up and down the queue by volunteers. Hills on the north bank rose high enough to stand as a promise of the Highlands, toward which many of the motorists were headed. At other stopping places – ferries, scenic spots, ruins and castles – they would come across more bagpipers, other conscientious daughters urging them to part with a few pennies. They were like a secret population, these bagpiping people.

'Four years back,' said Ashton, 'there was a piper who took up a pitch on the north shore. He'd no license for it, so the police moved him on, and thank God for that. There were bagpipes there and bagpipes over there, and in the middle of the very river the two wails met, and the racket made your hair stand on end. No kidding,' he said. 'It made my teeth itch. I hate bagpipes. They remind me of the Army.'

'Somehow,' Jim said, 'I thought you were in the Navy.'

'Funnyman, aren't you?'

'It's the way you talk, Ashton. 'Port' this, 'starboard' that, 'amidships' –'

'I've been watching you, and I've noticed. Don't think there's a lot goes on here that Wattie Ashton doesn't see. I've seen you, sitting on that wall, and I've seen the way you look at that tinker's daughter.' Ashton nodded, approving of his own moral malevolence. 'Call yourself educated?'

Over and back again, over and back again – north bank, south bank, north bank, south bank; with each crossing of the broad river, Jim's hands grew dirtier with the feel of copper coins. Ink and paper from his roll of tickets added to the grime on his fingers, the palms of his hands, creeping up as far as his wrists. Rain clouds massed over Dumbarton Rock, which rose around the bend of the river like a fortified stud on the belt of antique stones round Scotland's waist – Dumbarton, Stirling Castle, Edinburgh Castle. The clouds were dark enough to warn of a summer downpour. It rained that day, and made the work miserable and wet. From the top deck, he saw Robertson and the girl under a tree.

On a Friday evening, having just been paid, Jim took a silver florin from his wage packet and dropped it into the girl's pouch as he passed her. A few seconds later, it bounced off the road in front of him. He saw it roll under a car. He turned round, but she already had her back to him and was shaking her cloth bag at the cars. Robertson noticed, too, but he kept on piping.

'How come,' Jim asked his mother, 'Robertson's daughter would throw back at me the florin I dropped into her bag? I thought we were well in with the tinkers. I mean, free eggs, and my father fixes them up with jobs.'

'For someone who's supposed to have brains,' said Mrs Gilchrist, 'you're not very bright.'

'She threw it back at me,' he said angrily.

'Maybe she likes you,' his mother said. 'If I were a tinker lass whose father set her to begging off other folk and somebody I liked gave me a coin – more, maybe, than I was used to getting – then I think I'd throw it back.' She smiled as she watched Jim thinking about what she'd said. 'Don't do anything silly,' she went on. 'It'd be a great waste, you riding the length and breadth on a horse and cart.'

'She's practically a next-door-neighbour, and I don't even know her first name. She hasn't said a word to me. It's not like how you think,' he said. 'I'd just been paid, and I felt generous.'

'You so much as kiss her ear,' his mother said, 'and you'll wish you'd been stolen by the fairies. You, me, and your dad would find ourselves at a tinker's wedding – yours. They might look like nothing on earth, but they're very strict when it comes to what might be flitting across your mind.'

Throughout the remainder of the summer, Jim thought about how to speak to the girl. She seemed able to guess whenever he came close to working up the courage. Blank as her expression looked, it was an emptiness that had been brought up on conventions of hostility, and that prepared her for the exercise of that gruff, rude dignity with which she snubbed and avoided him. Every few days, he joined the Robertsons at their fire as they sipped their strong tea. The girl said nothing, and her father did not think it discourteous when she walked away to stand by herself.

'Where did you learn to play?' Jim asked the man.

'My uncle taught me. He was a famous piper. Much better than my father was.' Robertson groaned as he stood up. 'I can huff and puff like the big bad wolf,' he said, 'but it's hard on the legs.'

At the far end of the clearing, the girl counted the coins in her bag. Robertson doused the fire with what was left of his tea. He picked up his pipes and walked away. Before she followed him, the girl scuffed a foot's-worth of leaf mould on to the sizzles of the fire. She didn't even look at Jim. He felt inferior.

'Shy, aren't you?' said Ashton, back at the boat. 'Tongue-tied and bashful. You slow down, she gives you a bad look, and then she gets on wi' her begging. A beggar's what she is, isn't it? Don't you know it? She's as far away from your own kind as a duchess or Lady Mucky-Muck. Will you buy a ticket for a good cause?' He was selling raffle tickets for the Scotland-USSR Friendship Society. 'First prize is a week in Leningrad.'

'What's the second prize?'

'If that's your attitude, then you don't deserve the opportunity of a lifetime which a possible prize-winning ticket would put your way.'

'I suppose Poles and Hungarians get free tickets?'

'Counter-revolutionary trash gets what's coming to it, and that's what *it* gets. Forget it,' Ashton said. 'I can see I'm wasting time.'

On the morning that Robertson's band of tinkers were to leave for their autumn and winter camp, Jim turned up for work an hour early, at half-past six. Ashton was already on board. He scowled at Jim.

'What've I done wrong this time?' Jim asked.

'Nothing.' Ashton gave a shrug of innocence, his mouth opening, his teeth shining, amusement slowly drawing over his face. A late-September breeze nudged at Jim's cap as three tugs in a line went downriver. 'It's your last day, an' I'll be glad to see the back of you. It'll no' be like last year, or the year before. When you cross here in the morning to catch your bus to the university, don't expect any favours when it comes to your fare.'

'I've never heard you laugh, Ashton. When did you last laugh, like a normal person?'

'I laugh when I see a loser. I'm laughing right now.'

There was no sign of Robertson's convoy on the road. Jim said, 'The tinkers are crossing this morning. You listen, Ashton, and you listen good. They're going across, and no fares. If you make an issue of it, you'll wish you hadn't bothered.'

'So that's why you got here before the early-duty car man. Sorry to disappoint you,' Ashton said. He pointed to horse dung on the car deck. One of the piles had been trodden by heavy tyres. 'You being the Tinkers' Friend, I was waiting on you to clean it up. They went through here a good half-hour ago.' Ashton dragged on his cigarette, and his smoke trailed in the wind. 'Three horse-drawn vehicles, one lorry, eighteen passengers, six of whom were half-fare, them being underage. You're the man wi' the brain. You can tot that up in a flash, no bother, I'm sure. When did I laugh last? I've been laughing all morning. Here,' he said, handing Jim a shovel. 'Go and clean up what they left you.'

'Are you sure it was them?'

'I've been here since 1933. Would I not recognize them? I looked forward to telling that scabby piper no' to come back, him and his mangy clan. They're redskins, jumping the reservation. Sure I'm sure. I'd know them a mile away. Why do you think I got here early?'

The wash of a freighter slapped against the ferry and ran over the car deck. Withdrawing waves swept it clean. Jim handed the shovel back to Ashton.

'Where are you going now?' Ashton shouted.

'Up for'ard,' Jim shouted back, 'to wait for your brother. Full fare!'

THE CANOES

Peter and Rosalind Barker began their holiday on Loch Arn on an evening in the first week of August. We were standing by the rail of what is known in our village of Locharnhead as the Promenade – a name that does no more than repeat the intent of the old Duke, who paid for its construction many years ago as a means of employing our fathers. It is just a widening of the pavement by the side of the road that runs along the head of Loch Arn and then peters out in an unpaved track a mile farther on. We have ten yards of Promenade, and that is not much of a walk. Our fathers used to lean on a low stone wall there. Now, as the old Duke considered this wall a symbol of our fathers' idleness, the job of knocking it down for good wages was meant to be significant. As a boy, I remember the old Duke's rage when, within a day of the work's completion, as he found our fathers loafing on the splendid new barrier they had just built, he craned from the window of his big car and cursed them to lean perpetually on a hot rail by the hearths of damnation. On summer evenings, therefore, we stand where our fathers stood, and one or two very old men sometimes stand beside their sons. For the most part we keep our mouths shut and enjoy the mild breeze that whispers across the water.

The Barkers looked a prosperous young couple. Mr Barker could have been no more than thirty years of age; his wife might have been a year or two younger. Their skins were already tanned, which I thought strange for two people at the start of their holiday. Mrs Barker wore a broad red ribbon in her fair hair, and I was pleased to see that her husband was not the sort of young man whose hair hides his ears and touches his shoulders. They both wore those modern clothes that, in my opinion, look so good on young, slender, healthy men and women. And I noticed that they wore those useful shoes that have no laces but can just be kicked off without your stooping to struggle with ill-tied knots as the blood rushes to your head.

Mr Barker parked his car in the place provided by the County Council, adjacent to the jetty. The jetty was paid for by the old Duke. It is announced as Strictly Private Property on a wooden notice board, though few people here can be bothered to read notices. The paint has long since peeled from it, and its message is rewritten in the badly formed letters of the new Duke's son's factor: Perhaps more would be done for the attractions of Locharnhead, which stands in need of a coat of paint throughout, if it was not the sort of place you can only get back from by returning along the arduous way you came.

Our eyes swung genially to the left to inspect the new arrivals – all, that is, except those of Martin MacEacharn, who is so dull of wit he proclaims himself bored with the examination of tourists. They are a kind of sport with the rest of us. Much amusement has been given to us by campers and hikers and cyclists in their strange garbs and various lengths of shorts and sizes of boots. We tell them they cannot light fires and pitch their tents where they are permitted to do so; and we tell them they may light fires and pitch tents to their hearts' desire where gamekeepers and bailiffs are guaranteed to descend on them once it is dark and there will be no end of inconvenience in finding a legal spot for the night.

Young Gregor remarked enviously on the couple's motorcar. It was low to the ground, green, sleek, and new, and obviously capable of a fair rate of knots. Magee, whose father was an Irishman, ambled over toward Mr and Mrs Barker, pretending he was too shy to speak to them. They were admiring the fine view of the long loch from the jetty. Mr Barker had his arm around his wife's shoulders and was pointing to various phenomena of loveliness in the scenery. They are a familiar sight to us, these couples, who look and behave as if they feel themselves to have arrived in a timeless paradise of water and landscape and courteous strangers in old-fashioned clothes. On fine summer evenings the stillness of the water may be impressed on all your senses to the abandonment of everything else. Our dusks are noted far and wide and remembered by all who have witnessed them. On Loch Arn at dusk the islands become a mist of suggestions. There are old songs that say if only you could go back to them once more, all would be well with you for ever.

Mr Barker noticed Magee beside him and said, 'Good evening,' which Magee acknowledged with his shy smile and slow, soft voice. 'You'll be looking for me, perhaps,' Magee said. All of us leaning on the rail of the Promenade – Muir, Munro, Young Gregor, MacMurdo, MacEacharn, and myself – nodded to each other. When the couple saw us, we all nodded a polite and silent good evening to them, which we believe is necessary, for they have heard of our courtesy, our soft-spoken and excellent good manners and clear speech. All except Martin MacEacharn extended them the thousand welcomes; he was undoubtedly thinking too hard in his miserable way about the Hotel bar behind us and for which he had no money to quench his thirst.

'If you're the boatman, then, yes, you're the man we're waiting for,' said Mr Barker to Magee. My, but he had a bright way of saying it, too, though we all thought that a couple who possessed two long kayak canoes on the trailer behind their motorcar had no need of a boatman. He towered over Magee, who is short, wizened, bowlegged, and thin, though his shoulders are broad. Mrs Barker, too, was a good half foot taller than him.

'Well, I think I can just about more or less manage it,' said Magee, with a quick look at his watch, which has not worked in years. 'Yes,' he said, for he must always be repeating himself, 'just about. Just about, if we're handy-dandy.'

'Handy-dandy?' said MacMurdo with contempt. 'Where does he pick them up, for goodness' sake?'

Magee, as we all knew, was desperate for a bit of money, but a lethargic disregard of time is obligatory in these parts. Or that, at least, is the legend. What I will say is that if Magee is late for his dinner by so much as half a minute, his wife will scatter it, and probably Magee as well, before her chickens. Social Security keeps him and the rest of us alive, and I have yet to see a man late for his money. If it ever came to the attention of the clerk that Donal Magee turns a bob or two with his boat, then he would be in deeper water than the depths of Loch Arn, some of which, they say, are very deep.

It soon became clear why the Barkers couldn't paddle themselves out to Incharn. Gear and suitcases are awkward to transport by canoe. Magee, a lazy man, turned round to us with a silent beckoning. He was asking us to lend him a hand but was frightened to say so aloud for fear that our refusals might ruin the atmosphere of traditional, selfless welcoming he had created with such skill and patience. We turned away with the precision of a chorus line it was once my good fortune to see in one of these American musical films – all, that is, except Martin MacEacharn, who wasn't looking.

Once Magee had loaded his boat and tied the canoes to its stern, the flotilla set off in the dusk like a mother duck followed by two chicks. I treated them to one of my lugubrious waves, which I am so good at that no one else is allowed to make one while I am there. How many times, after all, have the holiday types said to us, 'We will remember you forever'? It is a fine thing, to be remembered.

Incharn is a small and beautiful island. That, at any rate, is how I remember it, for I have not stepped ashore there since I was a boy. A school friend of mine, Murray Mackenzie, lived on Incharn with his mother and father. Only one house stands there among the trees, with a clearing front and back, between the low knolls at each side of the small island. When the Mackenzies left for Glasgow, or whatever town in the south it was, Murray was given a good send-off at school. We had ginger ale, sandwiches, and paper streamers. The minister of the time presented him with a Holy Bible, in which we all inscribed our names in their Gaelic forms.

For a good few years the house lay empty. None of the Duke's men were inclined to live there and put up with rowing back and forth on the loch to get to work and come home from it. A childless couple took its tenancy. The man was a forester, and every day he rowed his boat to a little landing stage by the loch side and then followed the steep track over the hill. But his wife was visited by another boat, at whose oars sat Muir's elder brother, a self-confident and boastful lad who had spent four years at sea with the P & O Steam Navigation Company. Still, the poor woman must have been lonely on Incharn, all by herself most of the day, and she would have grown sick of it, especially in winter, waiting for her man to row back in the early dark; and it would have been worse if there had been a wind blowing or a bad snow. Muir's elder brother went back to sea without so much as a farewell to his fancy woman, and he has never been heard of since. She was found by her husband, standing up to her middle in the waters by the pebble beach, shivering and weeping but unable to take that last step – and one more step would have been enough, for it shelves quickly to the depths. They, too, left, soon after that, and the island and its house lay empty. To row past it used to give me the shudders. I was a young man then, and had been away, and would go away again.

For a number of years the house has been rented in the summer months. The Duke's factor will accept only those who are highly recommended by the solicitor in London who handles the Duke's English business.

Magee and his hirers were soon no longer visible to the naked eye. We lounged by the rail, which has been rubbed by our hands and elbows to a dull shine. Muir, I think, remembers his lost brother when he looks toward Incharn, though he is too sullen to say so.

'Another couple to Incharn, then,' said Munro. 'Now, there's been more folk through the door of that house in a couple of years than there have been kin of mine through the door of my mother's house.' He always calls his house his mother's. She has been dead for twenty years; but we are born in houses, as well as of mothers.

'It's a sad thing that no one will lend a man the price of a pint of beer,' said MacEacharn.

'If we wait for Magee returning,' said the cool, calculating, and thirsty MacMurdo, 'then we'll have the price of several apiece. A twenty-minute drag over the loch is worth a pound or two.'

'Aye,' said Young Gregor, 'and don't forget the twenty minutes back.'

Eyes tried to focus on Incharn as its form vanished into the dusk. Lips were wetted by tongues as we imagined the pints of beer to which Magee might treat us on his return if we behaved nicely toward him or threatened him with violence. But Magee was in one of his funny moods. He is not the man to stand up to a woman like his wife. Munro has said, 'I'm glad I am married to the woman who accepted my proposal, but I'm doubly thankful I'm not married as much as all *that*.'

Magee did not come back but illustrated once again how he has inherited from his father an aptitude for the evasion of responsibilities. He beached his boat a few hundred yards to the right of us, where there is a spit of sand, and then went home in the dark with his money, hoping perhaps to buy a few hours of peace and quiet through giving his wife a cut of his boatman's fee.

That Magee had been well paid is a matter of which I am certain. A couple of nights after the arrival of Mr and Mrs Barker, I had nothing to do, and Magee agreed that I go with himself and another English couple to Inverela, where there is another house on the new Duke's son's estates. It stands by the loch side and cannot be reached by road unless you park a mile from it and then walk along a narrow track. To go by boat is only sensible.

'Well, well, then,' Magee began as we were taking our leave of the Englishman on Inverela's tiny landing stage. His wife, by the way, was running around cooing about how wonderful it was, but we took no notice of that. 'I hope the weather stays fine and the loch remains as calm as a looking glass all the while you are here.' Highly impressed by this eloquent desire for their comforts, the Englishman gestured for his wife to come over and hear this, because it was obvious that Magee was far from finished. 'And may there be no drop of rain, except perhaps once or twice in the night, to make your mornings fresh and to keep the leaves as green as you wish to see them.' They settled back before this recitation. 'And may your sleep be undisturbed and tranquil and you have no reminder whatsoever of the cares of the world, which I am told are the very devil outwith of Loch Arn. And, to translate from our Gaelic' – of which Magee knows one curse, two toasts, and a farewell – 'may your bannocks never freeze over or your hair fall out, and may you never forget to salt your potatoes.'

I imagined how that couple would say to each other, as soon as our backs were turned, that it was true after all: the people here speak better English than the English. In that matter, the explanation is to be found in the care with which our kinsmen of long ago, in their clachans by the shores of Loch Arn, set about forgetting their original tongue so that their children, and their children's children, and all their posterity would converse in translation.

As Magee stepped into his boat, it was in the way of a man who expects to be paid nothing at all for his troubles. His grateful employer was shuffling in his jacket for money – a sight studiously avoided by Magee's little blue eyes, which are too close together. The Englishman had a look of prosperity about him and a willingness to be forthcoming. 'Ah . . . ah . . .' The Englishman was a bit embarrassed. 'How much do I owe you?'

Now, there can be a long and historical answer to that one, but Magee thought for a moment with one hand on his chin while the other removed his hat and began scratching his head. 'How . . . how much would you say it was worth?'

'Would a fiver do?' said the Englishman. His wife nudged him. Magee, like myself, was quick to notice that this woman, in a hat of unduly wide brim – dressed, it seemed to me, for a safari – was a touch on the overpaying side of humanity.

I was all for putting an end to Magee's playacting and stretching my own hand out to receive the note. But Magee began ponderously calculating: 'Now, then . . . It is thirty minutes out, after the ten minutes it took to get you aboard, and unloading you took another ten minutes, while it will take us another thirty to get back home . . .'

That was a fine stroke of obscurity, for the man was nudged once more by his grinning wife, and he produced another fiver. Two fivers together was more than the government gave you for having no job. Magee looked at the notes as if insulted. 'Now, that seems a lot to a man like myself . . . sir,' he said. 'How does the seven pounds strike you . . . sir? You see, it's the fair price.'

'A bit of a problem there,' said the gent. 'I haven't a single note on me.'

'Then, in that case,' said Magee, a bit too quickly, 'I'll take the ten pounds and I'll see you when you come to Locharnhead.'

'How will we get there?' asked the woman, who was already blinking in a soft hail of midges.

'By that boat there,' said Magee, who pointed to a beached rowing boat that belonged to the house. 'Or you may walk by the track, on your right.'

'Ah. I see. Yes, indeed. On the right, you say?'

'On the right, sir. But you will be quicker by the loch.'

I remember it took the Englishman four hours to row to Locharnhead the following day, for that canny son of an Irishman had been to Inverela that morning to hide one of the oars. Magee did well with a sort of contract for their subsequent transportation.

'Ten pounds for a night's work, Magee,' I said on our return voyage. 'Is it not a liberty to take so large a sum, even from an Englishman who looks as though he can well afford it?'

'Do you want a drink?' he asked. 'Or do you want a *good* drink?'

'You know me,' I said.

'Then hold your hush and don't whine at me for a hypocrite. Because daylight robbery is exactly what it is, and you and the rest of them will sup on the benefit of it. Though I'll tell you true enough that if he didn't look such a pig of a rich man in his pink shirt and white breeks, I'd have let him off with the three pounds the factor says is the fixed charge to Inverela.'

We passed Incharn on the return trip in the late dusk. I waved to its holiday tenants, who had lit a fire on the beach. That couple we'd just left at Inverela could not be imagined lighting a bonfire. I had a feeling the Barkers would have been glad of our company if we had called on them for a few moments, but the thirsty lads, we knew, would be waiting for us on the Promenade, and with me in the boat Magee would have no chance of getting up to his tricks. In the light of their bonfire Mr and Mrs Barker looked like people of the far long ago, when, we are told, there was great happiness and heroism in the world. Or it may just have been the way they carried their youthfulness that led me to think so.

'Now, I hope you didn't fleece that nice couple of the Barkers there.'

'What kind of a thief do you take me to be? I asked for the factor's fixed charge, and they were kind enough to pass me a fiver.'

'Aye, well, there will be no more work for you out of that pair. These two are water babies.'

A day or two later I was walking on the hill. My old pal Red Alistair was, I knew, reluctantly laying down a drain on the Duke's lower pastures – the one he was meant to do the year before but didn't get around to finishing. He is called Red on account of the political pamphlets he inherited from his father. He is annoyed by the nickname, being twice the Tory even than the new Duke's son, and he keeps his legacy of pamphlets in deference to his father's memory. As I was looking for Red Alistair, I found the minister scrutinizing the loch through his spyglass.

'Now, there's a sight I've never seen on the loch before,' he said. 'There are two canoes on it today.'

He gave me his glass and I had a clear view of Mr and Mrs Barker in single line ahead. They wore yellow waterproof jackets and sensible life jackets as well, which was a relief to me.

'Is there any chance of that becoming popular?' I asked the minister, after I had told him who the two canoeists were and what nice people they had turned out to be.

'You should ask that of Young Gregor. He's the boy who's daft on boats round here, though if he ever opens that marina he does nothing but talk about, we will become a laughing-stock for our broken craft, and make no mistake.'

He was as disappointed in Young Gregor as we all were. 'Go, for God's sake, to a southern city,' we urged the boy. 'There's nothing here but old men and the bed-and-breakfast trade.' Lack of capital was what he complained of – that and the poor show of enthusiasm he received from the manager of the Bank, which comes twice a week to Locharnhead in a caravan.

'These canoes can fairly shift some,' said the minister. 'My, if I was young, I'd be inclined to try my hand at that. What an emblem of youth is there before our eyes.'

'We should encourage Young Gregor in it,' I suggested. 'These craft appear to have no engines at all.'

'That boy will break my heart. Is there nothing that can be found for him to do?'

'Can you imagine any woman from round here sporting about on the water like that?'

'Our women are not so much bad-natured as unpredictable,' he decided. 'By and large, though, it might be the bad nature you cannot predict. But we have known great joys in our time. There is no sweeter thing in this life than an harmonious domesticity. You know, I even miss the bad nature of my late wife.' He paused as he peered through his telescope. 'They are a tall couple, these English Barkers.'

'They tell me she is called Rosalind.'

'Now, that is a name from Shakespeare, I believe.'

'Then it's a fair English name,' I remember saying, 'for a young woman as handsome as Mrs Barker and with a true demeanour to go with it.'

'It makes a change from Morag, or Fiona, I'll say that much,' said the minister.

For many more minutes we stood there on the hill, exchanging the spyglass as we watched the two canoes.

'What day is it?' asked the minister.

'I think it must be Thursday, for I saw the women waiting on the fishmonger's van.'

Mr and Mrs Barker visited the Hotel bar in the early part of some evenings for a drink and a bite to eat. While they were inside, we took the opportunity of examining their Eskimo craft – not, of course, that there is much to look at in a kayak canoe. I studied them longer than the others had the patience for. A jaunt in one of them would have been very satisfying. To have asked Mr Barker might have been thought a bit eccentric of me, though I doubt if he would have taken it as an impertinence. Their canoes had a very modern look to them, as, indeed, had that bright and lively couple with their air of freedom.

'Aye,' said MacMurdo, who joined me on the jetty, 'that must be a fine and healthy outdoor sport for them – the sort of thing that could set you up for the winter and keep you well.' MacMurdo, fresh-faced as he is for his years, is housebound for three months of the calendar with the sniffles. When the Barkers came back, we stood to one side and said our soft 'Good evening' together, which they returned. Then we watched them slip into their canoes and paddle away into the early dusk.

'It's the best time of all to be on the water,' said MacMurdo. 'Just look at the beauty of it over there. The whole world is getting itself ready to settle down for the night.'

'Do you think he'd mind if I asked him – I mean, if he'd let me take his canoe out for a few minutes?'

'What's so special about one of these canoes?'

'They strike me for one thing as an exciting little sort of a craft, that's what. Now, look there, and see how close you would be to the water.'

'A man of your age . . . A boat like that is for young things.'

'It would be interesting to *me*.'

* * *

A man like myself might be expected to resent these folks who come up from the south like the swallows to take their ease on a country that has brought me no prosperity. All the same, no one can tell me better than I tell myself that I am as lazy as any man born. Part of my trouble is that I have become content enough on plain victuals in modest quantities and two packets of Players a week. What jobs I've done in other parts than this one did not contribute much to my happiness. But there are things I've seen, and people I've met, I would not do without if I had my chance again. When the mobile library, which is a wonderful thing, calls at Locharnhead, I am the first man aboard and the last man out. That is not hard, as the only other reader in our community, apart from the youngest MacMurdo when he's at home, is Mrs Carmichael, wife of our stingy publican and the Hotel's cook. By the way, I once ate a large dinner there. It was not worth the money, and Magee and the rest of them watched me through the window for all five courses, screwing up their faces and licking their chops in an ironic manner. MacEacharn, I noticed, was there, too, but that obstinate man wasn't even looking.

But for all the large contrast between myself and the likes of Mr and Mrs Barker, it made me mellow and marvellously sad to watch them paddle in the still waters of Loch Arn at dusk, going toward Incharn, where the Mackenzies once lived, and that unhappy couple who followed them.

Incharn, as I have said, is a beautiful island. A good number of trees grow there, and on the side you cannot see from the head of the loch there is low ground and a growth of reeds of which nesting swans and water-fowl are appreciative. This is the most beautiful side of all, though you can only see it properly from the water, which means that it has been observed by few people. Facing Locharnhead, the beach is of fine pebbles, and it slopes quickly into the water. Crab apples grew there when my friend Mackenzie lived on it, and that bitter fruit made grand jelly in his mother's big copper pan. They had a black leaded stove of great size, which Mrs Mackenzie kept as spotlessly black as a Seaforth's boots, and we were famous for the spit and polish. Mrs Mackenzie would do her washing in a wooden tub on the beach, and her suds floated and spread as Murray and I threw stones at the scattering patches of foam. People on holiday do no washing at all, I'm told. Sometimes I felt like telling Mr and Mrs Barker about Incharn, but I never got round to it. They might have been interested. Magee has been known to tell those he ferries to the island of the tragedy that befell there. In his story, the woman drowned herself, and her demented husband first slew her lover with his bare hands and then committed his own life to the chill waters, but it was not that way. For all I know, the Barkers heard that story from Magee; but if they did, they were too happy to pay it any heed.

At night you can see the small lights of the cottage if its blinds or curtains are not drawn. In our famous dusks and sunsettings, the lights seem to spread in the open and watery mist, and they float above the island like benedictions. A man can look toward Incharn and feel drawn toward it. Muir's brother may have felt that, too, for whether the beauty of a place discriminates among those who are to be compelled by it is not a subtlety I am prepared to go into. Incharn draws a charitable thought from me, at any rate. But then I was always a bachelor, though not because I wanted to be one; and so I am always glad of something that holds disgruntlements at bay. All winter long I look forward to the holiday couples. It would please me more if Mr and Mrs Barker were to come back, with their frail canoes, and the way they splashed each other with water off their paddles, and capsized and rolled over under the water and came back up again as my heart beat with admiration for them – and, above all, the way they just followed each other about on the still water.

BOBBY'S ROOM

Henry Pollock was the only child of only children, and his four grandparents were dead. When he was twelve, in 1954, he and his parents left Glasgow on a motoring holiday. They stayed in a succession of hotels all over the Borders and the southwest of Scotland. At one place, they found that the hotels and guest-houses were full. It was a town Mrs Pollock particularly wanted to visit, and all the rooms were booked up for some local annual event. Mr Pollock was irate. His wife chided him for not having telephoned a reservation in advance, as, she said, she had suggested in the first place.

'We said potluck was part of the charm, did we not?' was Henry's father's riposte. Bickering in the car park lasted almost an hour.

Pollock was a tall man, powerful, proud, and successful; Henry had got used to his obstinate refusals to give in to his wife's complaints or preferences, to which, in the end, he always conformed without seeming to surrender. Harsh words when they fell out were, Henry knew, a prelude to that kind of morning on which he didn't see them until it was nearly noon. If these were mornings when he went to school, then his mother hurriedly threw his breakfast together and kissed him on the ear before running back upstairs in her kimono.

Even in the small space of the car, they managed to ignore Henry, and he knew better than to say anything.

'If you're in such a hurry to find somewhere, then why don't you drive?' his father asked Mrs Pollock.

'You know I can't. Don't be so stupid.'

'Then allow me to the judge of when we leave and when we don't. I need petrol, in any case.'

'You can't possibly need petrol. You filled up this morning in Dumfries.'

Eventually they got under way again, and after a few miles Pollock stopped the car outside a substantial stone-built villa, a house much like their own back in Glasgow; a notice board advertised that it offered accommodations.

'What do you think?' he asked.

'I think it's seen better days, that's what I think,' said Mrs Pollock, who was still simmering. Her husband went to see if there were two rooms available, and to investigate what the place was like. 'It doesn't even have a drive,' she said to Henry. 'Where will we put the car?'

'I don't see any cars,' Henry said, 'so they must have rooms.'

'When I want your opinion, I'll ask for it. *Netherbank*,' she said, sounding the name of the house as proof of its unsuitability.

Pollock returned a few minutes later. 'It's first-rate,' he said with genuine enthusiasm, leaning into the car. 'The rooms are large and spotlessly clean, very airy and spacious, and no one else is staying there.' Breezily, he listed the qualifications Mrs Pollock always insisted were necessary for a night's comfort. 'We can have the sitting room to ourselves, if we want it, and you'll find the bathroom highly acceptable. I think we should take it. Irene, it's run by a lovely old couple. You'll adore them.'

Netherbank was run by a Mrs Bawden. She was over sixty, silver-haired, round, short, respectable, and as Mrs Pollock said afterwards, very nicely spoken. She took it in her stride when Mrs Pollock asked if she could have a look at what she was offering for dinner. 'Normally, I prefer a proper restaurant. But my husband's very tired after a day's driving.'

'Some people ask me for what they call an 'evening meal' ,' Mrs Bawden said, lifting the lid off a saucepan. 'I call it dinner. I've always called it dinner, and I won't change now. Round about here, people call lunch dinner. But I call it luncheon, and I call it luncheon at twelve-thirty. And I call tea tea. I don't know where we'll all end up if we begin to call things by the wrong names.' Mrs Pollock couldn't agree more.

They stayed for five nights. Henry knew one of the reasons his parents liked the place so much: Mrs Bawden was very obliging. Before Mrs Pollock could ask, Mrs Bawden offered to keep an eye on Henry if they wanted to go off by themselves for a day, or go to dinner in a hotel restaurant about ten miles away which Mrs Bawden had heard was outstanding for its seafood. 'But Mrs Bawden, you'll do yourself out of business,' his mother said.

'No, no, I won't. You're on holiday, and it'll be my pleasure to help you enjoy yourselves.' Mrs Pollock revelled in being the beneficiary of that sort of consideration. Henry's parents had three days on their own without him, and three evenings at the famous restaurant.

Henry wandered round the hills and farms, and walked the two miles to the sea. He read, and he watched Mr Bawden at work in his garden. The old man was hard of hearing, or said he was, and when Henry tried to talk to him he pointed to an ear, smiled, and went back to his weeding or hoeing.

These were the last days of their holiday. His parents loved it. 'I haven't felt so refreshed and well in years!' said Henry's mother as they drove home. 'And Mrs Bawden – what a wonderful woman! Her cooking's pre-war! We were lucky to find it. It's the sort of place you could drive right past without giving it so much as a moment's notice.' After that, she and her husband looked at each other in the way that made Henry feel he wasn't there. A little later, Mrs Pollock started to sing. She coaxed Henry to join in. When he didn't, she turned round and said, 'You'll grow up to be miserable. Why won't you sing, like the rest of us?'

Two years later, there was a week in early June when Henry's father was more thoughtful than usual. After dinner he did a lot of meditative gardening. Tired of that, he sat in the lounge with an open book on his lap. Henry's mother brought him tea or coffee, asked him if he wanted something stronger, or something to eat, and in her busy efforts to leave him alone made a nuisance of herself. It was obvious to Henry that his father was making his mind up about something important. From time to time he saw his parents talk quietly and seriously to each other. They cuddled in the kitchen even more often than usual.

'Why don't I phone her? I kept a note of the number, you know,' he heard his mother say one evening.

'Do you think she would?' Pollock asked her. 'It's not really what she does.'

'Almost three months at her usual rates is probably very good business for her, especially if we add something on for her trouble. I imagine she'll be only too pleased.'

'It'd be ideal. But what do we do about the weeks of school he'll have to miss?'

'Darling, I've no intention of being left behind. It's an opportunity to travel I won't let pass by, especially since the offer specifically includes me as well. It's not as if you'll have to fork out for my fare and hotel bills. Some of us were prevented from travelling by the war, you know, not to mention marriage and motherhood.'

'If this trip's successful, there will have to be others, as a matter of course. It's a big project. It's not one bridge, it's a network. I don't look forward to going away without you, and I want you to come with me. But the best thing might be to start thinking about boarding school.'

'Were Henry younger, I'd say no, naturally. But at his age boarding school is probably a very adventurous proposition. I know it was for Alice Wylie's brother.'

Later that evening, Henry heard the telephone being used. He looked down into the hall from the top of the stairs and saw his mother leaning against the opposite wall while his father spoke into the phone. She was smoking, which she did only in company to be polite, or when she was agitated. Then she, too, went over to the phone and began to speak into it. Later, his mother called him to come down to the sitting room.

'Your mother and I have to go to Singapore,' his father said. 'We'll be gone for most of July and all of August and September. And I'm afraid it just isn't practical to take you with us.'

'You remember Mrs Bawden, and Netherbank?' His wife spoke sooner than Pollock would have liked. 'We've arranged for you to stay with her.'

'What about school?' Henry's tone of voice was meant to suggest that weeks of missed classes could be disastrous.

'Henry, you're the last person I can imagine slipping behind. A few weeks won't be a setback to you.'

His mother's way of speaking to him, her confidence in his maturity and academic excellence, made Henry want to fight back. He felt inclined to be stubborn and obstructive. 'There isn't a lot to do at Mrs Bawden's,' he said.

'We both think it's ideal.'

'We've no choice but to leave you behind.' his father said. 'We'll be happier, much happier, knowing you're somewhere we can feel easy in our minds about.'

Henry looked at his mother, hoping she would understand that he expected her to stay behind with him. She said, 'I'll talk to the headmaster on Monday. You can arrange for your teachers to give you a programme of study. You can do it on your own – I'm sure you can. And if you think you can't, you're underrating yourself.' He knew enough about her to know that if at his age she had been given a 'programme of study' she'd have collapsed in tears.

Instead of making it difficult for them, he accepted it, and resigned himself. He knew why they had chosen Mrs Bawden and Netherbank. They had been happy there, and assumed that he had liked it, too. It was a place and a few days in their lives that meant something in their happiness. He wondered why they could continue to be so ignorant of his feelings. Mrs Bawden was not a complete stranger, but she was the next thing to it – the landlady of a guesthouse, a species his mother usually loathed.

'Don't feel unwanted,' his mother said. 'It would suit us better, much better, if you could come with us. But it isn't possible, so we have to make the best of it.'

When the time came, they drove him to Mrs Bawden's with suitcases, books, tennis racquet, binoculars, and field guides to the birds and wildflowers of the British Isles. Nature study was his mother's idea. 'When I get back, I want to find you thoroughly up to the mark in country life,' she said. 'It's a wonderful opportunity for you. I've always been opposed to townies.' He tried to think of what it was she craved so determinedly that it made a trip to Singapore necessary to her.

She wept as she said goodbye. Henry felt like weeping on his own account.

'I know you won't give Mrs Bawden any trouble,' she said. It was the wrong thing to have said. Obedient to the point of filial perfection, he had never given anyone the least bit of trouble in his life.

'How long does post take from Singapore?' Mrs Pollock asked her husband.

'Airmail,' he said. 'Pretty fast.'

'Then I'll write at least once a week, and I'll expect you to do the same,' she told Henry. With that, she left for the car, dabbing at her eyes with a handkerchief.

'You haven't left me your address in Singapore,' Henry said. Pollock had to call for Mrs Bawden to bring a piece of paper for him to write it down on. He was embarrassed, talking about rush, last-minute details, oversights.

Henry had reckoned on eating alone in the dining room, like any other guest, but he ate with the Bawdens in their kitchen. 'No aunts, no uncles,' said Mr Bawden, as the old couple explored Henry's family. 'So no cousins, either. No great loss, if you ask me. A big scatter of kin makes you feel guilty at not keeping in touch, which you can't do, you know, unless you're a man of means and leisure.'

'I've second cousins,' Henry offered.

'I was closer to two of my second cousins than to any of my first,' said Mrs Bawden.

'I've never met them,' said Henry.

'Singapore's a long, long journey,' she said, pushing a bowl of cauliflower towards him.

'Home-grown,' said Mr Bawden. 'We haven't eaten a tinned vegetable in twenty years.'

As he lay awake in bed, Henry pondered his affection for his parents, and decided it was becoming as distant and routine as his parents' love of him. They were his parents, therefore he loved them; he was their son, therefore they loved him – it was as mathematical as that. Co-operation between them was beginning to thin out, like the darkness in the triangle of dawn now at the top of the curtains. His mother prodded him to be the scholar of his class at school, and was proud of his examination victories; but she nagged him for being too studious and staying in when he should have been outside and complained of his lack of interest in sport. They expected him to be perfect, but they neglected him.

He had a different room from the one he had slept in two years before. It was at the front of the house, under the eaves; from its protruding window he could look at a small wedge of sea and the right-hand tip of an island that could be walked to at low tide over the sands. Darkness turned to a transparent grey, and objects in the room slowly became visible. Shelves in an alcove contained dozens of books of boyish interest – books on ships and the sea, the Empire, foreign countries, warlike history, wildlife, fishing, landmarks in engineering and exploration, most of them heavy and already obsolete. There was a home-made model warship on a chest of drawers. Pictures on the wall did not quite cover the cleaner paint left behind from those that had been taken down. His dressing gown, on the hook behind the door, looked like another person in the room. He imagined that the owner of the books was a long-lost son of the Bawdens, dead, probably, in the war.

'Was my room your son's?' he asked Mr Bawden, who pointed to his ear as Henry began to repeat his question.

'We thought you'd like it better than the rooms we let to the holidaymakers,' he said. 'Or *she* did. You'll find out,' he said, as if excusing himself in advance for any apparent lack of initiative on his part. 'Mrs Bawden is the boss round here. She wears the trousers.'

'Where is he?'

'I haven't the foggiest. Somewhere or other.' He jabbed his rake on the dusty ground. 'It's good soil for carrots. And there's no better earth for potatoes.'

'Is he dead?'

'Good God, no. What gave you that idea? All that's wrong with Bobby is that he's a bit wayward when it comes to writing letters. What made you think he was dead?'

Henry was embarrassed, and with no way of explaining himself. Mr Bawden shrugged and retreated into his deafness and gardening.

Mrs Bawden was obviously told of Henry's questions in the garden. At dinner she recounted Bobby's travels – his letters from Australia, where he had spent three years, the good job in Hong Kong he'd thrown up on a whim in order to go to Canada. 'We're about due a letter from him soon.'

'What's that?' her husband asked.

'I said we're about due a letter from Bobby.'

'I'll believe it when I see it,' said Mr Bawden.

When Henry offered to do Mrs Bawden's shopping, it seemed as if she had been expecting him to ask. She gave him a list, and he pedalled the two miles to the nearest shop on a bicycle that had been Bobby's.

A family of five moved in, and stayed for three nights. They were boisterous, but their liveliness appeared toned down out of respect for someone else's house. Mrs Bawden had that effect on people. Henry kept out of their way. When he came down to say good night, Mr Bawden, alone in the kitchen with a book, directed him to the guests' sitting room. He found Mrs Bawden there with the father and mother of the visiting family.

'And this is Bobby in his uniform,' she was saying.

'My, he's a fine-looking young man.'

'And here's another one, with some friends of his from the same ship.'

'I'm off to bed now,' Henry told her.

'Good night, Henry.'

He was disconcerted by the sight of Mrs Bawden on the sofa, with a guest on either side of her, showing photographs of her son to people she had never seen before and might never see again. There was an amiable candour in her affectionate disappointment in Bobby, and it jolted Henry, who saw it as a failure of reticence, an openness that compromised her loyalty to her son. Snapshots of her son were being touted to strangers and were symptoms of an unhappiness she was too proud to notice.

'Is it all right if I take a cup of cocoa upstairs with me?' he asked Mr Bawden.

'Help yourself,' said the old man. Henry boiled the kettle and opened the cocoa tin. 'What is it, through there?' Mr Bawden asked. 'Snapshots and airmail letters?'

'What?'

'My wife, what's she doing?'

'She's talking to the guests.'

'See any photographs?'

'I think she *is* showing them photographs.'

The old man went back to his book.

Henry wondered how Mrs Bawden selected the people who were treated to her photograph albums. Perhaps everyone was, and perhaps his parents, two years before, had been shown the same photographs, with the same pride, and had listened to the same reminiscences. He felt sure that the visiting couple would have asked who Henry was, and been told that his parents had gone to Singapore, that his father was a civil engineer, and that they had stayed at Netherbank and thought it an ideal place to board their son while they were away. 'You ought to come home, Bobby,' he said to the vanished son. 'Not only does your mother miss you, but she talks about you to people she hardly knows. Worse, she's probably talking about me.'

There was a visitors' book on the hall table. Besides putting down their names and addresses, guests over the years had written their comments in a column where remarks were invited. 'We had a wonderful time.' 'Smashing food!' 'Highly recommended!' 'Excellent.' Henry leafed back to two years earlier. 'First-class!' his mother had written, in her bold, clear, self-assured handwriting. It was characteristic of her. Any time they travelled by train, his mother made it clear that they went first-class as a matter of course, and that some people did not – never would, never could.

As soon as the family of five left, Netherbank was full almost every night. His parents had found the house to their taste because they had it to themselves, and they were lucky. People often had to be told that there were no rooms left.

Henry tried to keep away from the guests as much as he could, but it was impossible not to ask Mrs Bawden each morning if there was anything she wanted him to do. 'Maybe you don't think it's man's work,' she said, 'but I could fair do with someone to strip the beds this morning and bring the linen down here for me to launder.' As the days went by he found himself aproned, pulling linen from beds, vacuuming carpets, dusting furniture, cleaning windows and mirrors, polishing the bannister.

'Next time we hear from you,' said Mr Bawden, 'you'll be running a hotel. You've taken to it. But don't tell me you like it. Believe me, I know – no one better. She's a hard woman to refuse.'

A girl from Lincolnshire, about Henry's age, passed him in the hall and said, 'You must be blind. What's that, then, if it isn't carpet fluff? There,' and she pointed. Later the same morning, egged on by a friend who was along on holiday with that family, the girl asked him, 'Is this your career? Or is it a punishment?'

'Have you been very bad?' the other girl said, giggling.

'Shoo!' Henry waved a duster at them, and they ran away delighted and laughing.

Breakfast was at seven for the Bawdens and Henry, so that they could eat before the rush of holiday families to the dining room. 'The Abercrombie children are sleeping three to a bed,' said Mrs Bawden. 'I told Mr Abercrombie it was the best I could do, and he was only too pleased to accept. The English family are just the same. There'll be eighteen for breakfast. I've never been so busy.'

'Why folk go on holidays I'll never know,' said Mr Bawden.

'Do you want me to wait on the tables?' Henry offered.

Mr Bawden gave him an uncertain look, and shook his head in a gesture of subdued bewilderment. 'Eighteen,' he said. 'She could never cook and serve at the same time – not for eighteen.'

'You ask them what they'd like,' said Mrs Bawden, patting his hand appreciatively. 'We have fruit juice. We have porridge and packet cereals. This morning we have kippers, and we have eggs, bacon, sausages, and those who want a fried breakfast are to be asked if they want black pudding with it. Some don't like it, others love it. I never need to take a note, but it might be for the best if you were to write down the orders, like a proper waiter. Eggs scrambled, fried, boiled, or poached. Tea or coffee, and toast, jam or marmalade. And if someone high and mighty asks you for kedgeree, look daft and pretend you've never even heard of it.'

'Should I get changed?'

'Put on my big white apron and you'll look the part well enough. And don't be nervous. We're not the Ritz,' she said.

Mr Bawden slipped out into the garden with his second cup of tea.

Most guests chose to come down at eight-thirty, and within the space of a few minutes the dining room was full. Henry was surprised that they could be so fussy about what to eat.

'Are the sausages fresh?' a man asked.

'I can't see Mrs Bawden serving you a bad sausage, sir.'

'What's a black pudding?'

'Black pudding,' Henry said, with a hesitant shrug.

'But what's it made of?'

'Hold on.' He asked Mrs Bawden what black puddings were made of, and Mr Bawden, rinsing his cup at the sink, raised his eyebrows.

Henry came back from the kitchen. 'Blood and lights,' he said.

'I'll have two lightly poached eggs. No, wait a minute. Did you say there were scrambled eggs? In that case, I'll have scrambled eggs.'

The two girls from Lincolnshire giggled as Henry stood in his apron with his pad and pen poised. The mother ordered them to hurry up. The father looked seriously at Henry, as if he thought he had been up to something.

By ten o'clock, Henry and Mrs Bawden were alone in the kitchen, tired out and hot and sipping tea. 'My twenty-of-everything set of breakfast china came in handy,' she said. Most of it was stacked beside the sink. 'The Lord be thanked, nobody wants lunch. Rooms next, then laundry. I don't know what I'd do without you, Henry. Next year I'll have to get a village girl to come in.'

Mr Bawden appeared with the mail.

'It's another letter from your mother!' Mrs Bawden said. She gave it to Henry. 'Go on, read it.'

His mother's cadences were in every line. They had been here, there, and seen that and other things. They had developed a taste for Chinese and Malayan food, although they'd been a bit suspicious at first.

'Is it so private that you can't read it out to me?' Mrs Bawden asked. Her husband hurried outside with a cup of tea in one hand and his watering can in the other. 'Does she say anything about the climate this time?' she said, remembering the first letter. 'Have they got over that exhausting journey? I didn't like the sound of the airport at Karachi.'

He glanced through the rest of the letter, to make sure his mother hadn't written anything embarrassing, thinking that it was only to be expected that an old woman who showed her snapshots to all and sundry would take it for granted that a letter should be shared. He read out his mother's account of the strange food, the deliciousness of which his parents had come round to accepting, and the sightseeing. "Daddy's had to fly up to Penang for a couple of days, so I've been left on my own. Everyone's extremely kind, and I've been playing a very great deal of bridge but as yet no mah-jong, thank goodness. We've been out for dinner every night since we arrived, and I shall be quite plump when I see you next. We look forward to a quiet evening by ourselves. Our bungalow is bijou but not quite as colonial as I would have liked. I'm not very geographical, as you know, and I wasn't quite sure where Singapore was, but I know now, Henry, and I don't mind telling you that it's ABSOLUTELY TROPICAL. It was so nice of you to press a flower in your letter. It made me feel quite homesick.''

'What a nice young man you are for doing a thing like that,' said Mrs Bawden. She patted his hand. 'I knew it,' she said. 'I knew it'd be hot there.'

A girl from an Edinburgh family asked Henry if he played tennis. He said he did. She asked if there was a court. He told her where the nearest one was, two miles away in the village.

'I don't have anyone to play with,' she said. She didn't sound as if she wanted particularly to play with Henry.

Her mother appeared at the door of the sitting room. 'Are you coming with us, or are you staying behind?' The woman's voice stated these options firmly, and Henry recognized the predicaments of both girl and parents.

Mrs Bawden came to the sitting-room door.

'Have you asked him?' the woman said to her daughter.

'It's two miles away,' the girl said, meaning that the court was too far to be practical.

'We'll drop you off at the court,' said her father from inside, through a rustle of newspaper.

'You haven't had proper company for nearly a month,' Mrs Bawden said to Henry. 'Go and play tennis if you want. I can answer the door and do what needs to be done. I can manage well enough without you.'

He ran upstairs, changed, got his racquet and a box of tennis balls. When he came down, the family of three was waiting in the hall, and the front door was open. The breeze disturbed the potpourri in the bowl on the hall table.

'I'm told that your father and mother are in Singapore,' said the man when they were in the car. 'Very interesting,' he said. 'Very interesting.' Henry had the impression he had been vetted and found to be a suitable companion for the girl.

'What's your name?' he asked her as they strolled to the tennis court.

'Louise,' she said.

'I know what it's like. At least yours haven't gone to Singapore.'

'I wish they would.'

'My mother's forgotten something, and it probably hasn't dawned on her yet. I'll be fifteen in a couple of weeks and she won't be here.'

'It isn't much of a tennis court,' Louise said.

She got bored and sat down, ignoring Henry's tepid but ironic serves as they bounced close beside her. Looking at her, he thought that there might be two major ways in which only children could turn out: they became either super-obliging, obedient models of courtesy and good behaviour or, like Louise, rebelliously surly and aggrieved. He never allowed his own grievances to show, and doubted if he ever would.

'When did your father say he'd pick us up?'

'He didn't.'

'What do you think of Mrs Bawden?'

'She certainly doesn't have any secrets.'

'And Mr Bawden?'

'I didn't know there was one. I thought she was a widow.'

'No secrets?'

'I feel sorry for Bobby,' she said. 'I couldn't stand it if my parents talked about me like that.'

'She misses him,' Henry said charitably, although he was interested that Louise disapproved of Mrs Bawden's lack of reticence as much as he did.

'I think I'd like to travel,' Louise said. 'My father says that air travel will grow enormously in the next few years. I would like to be an air hostess.'

'It's Bobby's room I've got. I think I'd like him. I imagine myself talking to him. I ask him what he'd do in my circumstances.'

'And I suppose you get some sort of mysterious answer,' she said sarcastically. 'Do they have a gramophone in that house? I haven't heard a single decent record since we came away.'

'He doesn't say anything,' Henry said. 'But I see him winking at me. I don't know what it means. Do you ever try to figure out what your dreams mean?'

'Isn't there somewhere we can get lemonade or something?' she said peevishly. 'I'm parched.'

'We could buy some in the shop,' he said, 'but there isn't a café.'

'What a dump!'

'I don't think you like being in the country.'

'I don't like being with my parents. I'd rather be in the city with my friends. At least there's something to do.'

'Is your father coming back for us?'

'I doubt it. I think we're expected to walk.'

She was unsympathetic and, Henry decided, stupid. She was also unhappy. It was her unhappiness that made her interesting. Her dislikes, her petulant good looks, her tone of voice gave the impression she was festering on the edge of a bitter family insurrection. He wondered what his father had found appealing in his mother. Louise made him think that his mother might have been like her at that age, twenty years before, in the nineteen-thirties. All that would have been different was that other kinds of music, other friends were being missed.

They walked back slowly. When they reached Netherbank, Louise's father's car was parked outside with several others. Her parents were in the garden with the Bawdens. The clear light peculiar to Galloway seeped out of the hill and fields and met a great arc of early-evening light rising from the sea. Louise's parents were holding hands. Henry thought that if his parents had been there, too, he would have experienced a moment in which the significance of how people exist to each other was clear and unmistakable. People who mattered less clouded the issue. He pressed Louise's hand, but she pulled it away.

At mid-morning the following day, Louise's father said to Henry, 'Do you keep an address book? If you don't then you should. Everyone ought to. Say goodbye, you two,' he said, looking at Louise. Henry felt that Louise had given a glowing report of him to her parents, even though, in his company, she had been standoffish, pert, and sardonic. 'You should exchange addresses and keep in touch,' her father added. He was strangely open and affable.

Louise produced her address book, and Henry dictated his address to her.

'I think that's very nice,' said Mrs Bawden. 'I think it's so nice,' she said to Louise's mother, 'that young people should exchange addresses and keep in touch.'

Mr Bawden came in by the front door, surprised to find guests still in the house that late in the morning. He could hardly turn round and go out again and found himself in the company.

'They're exchanging addresses. Isn't that nice, John?' his wife said.

Mr Bawden smiled at his wife, with whose obsessive and candid garrulity he was very tenderly and very gently browned off.

'Write letters,' she urged Louise. 'Write letters and use the phone only when you have to. Letters are *much* nicer. You can keep letters, but you can't keep phone calls. Have you taken a note of Louise's address?' she asked Henry.

'My book's upstairs. I'll take it from the visitors' book.'

As Mrs Bawden went out of the front door with Louise's parents, Henry followed with Louise. 'We don't have to write,' he said.

'I'm not good at letters. If you write first, you'll have a wait for an answer.'

'I don't think I'll ever forget you,' he said, 'but I don't know if you'd understand why.' She looked at him, and laughed quietly, but she was complimented by a surprising remark that sounded serious and mature. Her wave from the departing car was curious and concerned.

Henry waved back, and then went upstairs to strip those beds that needed to be freshly made for the arrival of new guests in the late afternoon and early evening. He suspected that a time would come when his parents would regret the three months in which they had hived him off to the Bawdens. He thought about the crisis that his awakening independence would cause in their lives; still he doubted if when it arrived they would be able to trace it back to his weeks in that safe, homely, and respectable house, or to that quaint old couple who lived in daily expectation of a letter from their son Bobby, in whose room Henry slept.

SOMETHING FOR LITTLE ROBERT

Mrs Mure-Thompson looked at her watch and checked it against the clock on the kitchen wall.

'You really don't have to do this,' said Mrs Duncan, her housekeeper, who came in at nine in the morning and left in the early evening.

'If there's nothing I can buy you, when I do so want to give you a present, then please, Letty, no matter what you say, I insist I get something for little Robert.' She had a perfunctory way of being pleasant. Mrs Duncan shrugged with resignation and ran the cold-water tap on the cloth she was rinsing. Mrs Mure-Thompson said, 'I'm sure he'll enjoy it even if you don't.'

'Oh, I didn't mean that. I'm grateful, Madam.' It was 1954, in Scotland, and 'Madam' was no longer a necessary deferential form of address. But Mrs Duncan found 'Mrs Mure-Thompson' a mouthful. It sounded more submissive than 'Madam.' 'It's only that I don't expect a present.'

Plump and pale, Mrs Mure-Thompson went from vigour one day to prone uselessness the next. Charities, gardening, and the church might involve her for weeks on end. Suddenly she would cancel all her engagements and withdraw to her room. During these days of brave misery she wrote letters to her many friends in India, where Mr Mure-Thompson had once worked, and in South Africa, Edinburgh, and the Highlands. Mrs Duncan took them to the post. Mrs Mure-Thompson reread the classics of children's literature. She thought of writing a book for children herself.

While Mrs Mure-Thompson was upstairs putting on her coat, Mrs Duncan went into the living room and looked up the long drive for signs of her son, Robert. It was a few minutes past four o'clock, and the school would be out. Robert had been told to come directly from school to the Mure-Thompsons' house. Everyone knew the house, which was much grander than any other house in the district; it had been built just before the war, and looked as if it had reached the age when it could wear the ivy and other climbing plants that covered its white walls. There was no sign of Robert, but there was still time for him to be punctual.

Mrs Mure-Thompson reappeared, pulling on her gloves – her light-blue summer gloves, which conformed with the mild, rainy afternoons of that September, and with its blue evenings. The two women possessed that strength of character known as independence. They knew their minds were confident: Mrs Mure-Thompson in telling Mrs Duncan what to do, and Mrs Duncan in the right way of doing it. That, anyway, was how it looked. Mrs Duncan acquiesced in her role for the sake of her wages. For Mrs Mure-Thompson's benefit, as if out of kindness, Mrs Duncan agreed, without humility, to accept Mrs Mure-Thompson's superiority. She also knew that she was more than a housekeeper. She was almost, but not quite, a companion. She was a hired friend. Only Mrs Mure-Thompson was entitled to any degree of informality in this arrangement. But apart from the 'Madam' two or three times a day, Mrs Duncan spoke to her as she would to anyone else.

'That boy,' she said. 'He walks at the speed of toddle-bonny. And if I know him, he'll turn up looking as if he's walked through a hedge.'

'Robert is *very* reliable,' said Mrs Mure-Thompson – a flattering contradiction of his mother's opinion of him.

'You can bet your boots on that,' said Mrs Duncan. 'You can rely on me having to wash his hands and face for a start, before you can take him anywhere.'

'Do you think he'd like a sandwich before we go?'

'You'll have little enough time as it is.'

They heard scuffing shoes on the gravel path outside the kitchen door. Robert knocked as his mother went to open it. 'I thought as much,' she said on her way to the sink. She ran the tap and held a flannel under it. 'Come over here.'

Robert was ten. He stood with his head to one side while his mother wiped his face without taking off his school cap. She left the flannel in his hands for him to wipe them himself while she fetched a towel.

Mrs Mure-Thompson smiled. 'If you're quite ready now,' she said, 'then we'll go into town, shall we?' Robert nodded. 'I'll just get the car.'

'What kind of coat do you want me to get?' he said to his mother.

'You'd better leave that to her, son.'

'What if you don't like it when we get back?'

'Mrs M-T'll have good taste, son. God knows why, but she insists on buying us something. Now, you behave yourself. And don't you go and take advantage of her.' Mrs Duncan buckled and tightened the belt of his navy-blue school raincoat. She looked down at his socks. She sat back on her heels, smartening him up. 'What have I told you? Keep your socks *up*.' She pulled up the fallen sock.

'The elastic bites my legs.'

She wiped dirt from the toes of his shoes with her hand. Outside, they could hear the cautious exit of Mrs Mure-Thompson's little car from the garage. 'Go on, off with you, then,' she said. She kissed him on the cheek.

It was a fifteen-minute drive into town. 'This is where Jim Hogg crashed his van,' the boy said as they approached a narrow, humpbacked bridge. 'Willie Blair says Mrs Hogg'll not get any money, because Jim Hogg was drunk, as usual.'

'Really? Who told you?' she asked. Mrs Mure-Thompson was interested in the sad controversies of the district.

'Bertie Hogg's in my class.'

'How awfully disturbing.'

Robert sat up, turned round, and craned a look at the river. A long raft of small half-sunken metal landing boats had been left there by the American Army years before. 'They say the Americans forgot to take them home with them.'

'Robert, I don't think they actually *forgot*.'

'No?'

'No.' She laughed.

'You haven't been in bed for a while.'

'I've been really quite well, thank you. Quite well.' Robert wondered why she didn't have much of a Scottish accent. 'Touch wood,' she said, 'but I've been in very good spirits.'

'I've had a cold.'

'I know, my dear. Did you get the book I sent you?'

'Yes, thank you. I sent you a note.'

'Of course you did!' Mrs Mure-Thompson was sincerely embarrassed. 'It was very kind of you to write to me.'

'I liked it. I really liked it.'

'One day,' she said, 'I'll write one myself. I'm sure I could do it. Do you think I could do one as good? Do you think I could write one as good as *The Little White Horse*?'

Robert had heard his mother talk to his father about Mrs Mure-Thompson's ambition to write a book for children. 'Can I read it when you've finished?'

'Will you tell me what you really think of it? Will you give me your honest opinion if I let you read it?'

'I can't read your handwriting,' he confessed, remembering the note that had come inside his illness book.

'I'll have you know,' she said, 'that I can type very well.'

Mrs Mure-Thompson negotiated her little car against the kerb in High Street outside Buchanan's Drapers, Haberdashers, and Outfitters. It was a shop that Mrs Duncan did not patronize. 'Don't see anything in there you like,' he remembered his mother warning his father and himself, 'because we can't afford it.'

The windows displayed farmerly tweed jackets, sombre suits, and stacked bolts of cloth. Slim imitation ladies, looking a little like young schoolteachers, wore tartan skirts, knitwear, and brown brogues with serrated tongues. One or two wore evening dresses, and one a wedding dress. Rosy-cheeked boys and girls, their waxen knees slightly chipped, advertised the uniform of the school in the town which, Robert had heard, you had to pay to get into if you were not so wonderfully clever that they could hardly refuse you.

They went into the large shop. A boy younger than Robert was sitting on the counter nearest the door and was softly drumming his heels against the dark brown varnish of the counter's wooden front. A woman assistant, wearing the regulation black twin-set and pearls for Buchanan's female staff, was expertly measuring yards of material from a large bolt. She stretched each length of cloth against the polished brass rule inlaid on the edge of the counter. 'No. Before you cut it,' said the boy's mother, as if about to change her mind, 'I'd like to see it in the daylight.'

A man approached Robert and Mrs Mure-Thompson, who had been waiting inside the door as if expecting someone to meet her. 'How nice to see you,' the man said. He smiled at the boy, suspecting he was the real customer. 'It's always a pleasure to see you, Mrs Mure-Thompson. Children's Department?'

'This is Robert,' she said, putting her hand on his shoulder, 'my housekeeper's son. And he would very much like to see what coats you have.'

'Mr Davidson,' said the assistant who had been measuring the cloth. Her posture and her voice were aggressively plaintive. 'Madam, here, would like to see this in the street, and the bolt's too heavy for me to carry. Would you, please?'

'One moment, Mrs Mure-Thompson.' Mr Davidson was displeased. He carried the bolt to the doorway and then, on the customer's instruction, out to the pavement. The assistant behind the counter sighed with late-afternoon exhaustion. 'My arms are fair hangin' off,' she said to Mrs Mure-Thompson, 'what wi' fetchin' an' carryin' bolts of cloth all day. I could do wi' a smoke.'

'Yes, thank you. I think I will have this,' said the customer to the worn-out assistant as Mr Davidson dumped the heavy bolt back on the counter.

'Sonny, don't kick the counter,' Mr Davidson said, discreetly severe, to the bored little boy who was sitting on it. 'Mrs Mure-Thompson,' he announced, with considerable self-aggrandizement, ushering her towards something much more pleasant than the unwanted interruption he had just taken in his stride.

They tried as many of the coats as would fit Robert. He did not like shopping for clothes. Fortunately, he didn't have to very often; but he hated being asked if things fitted here or were too big there, or if he liked the look of them. This time he found himself entering into the spirit of the occasion.

'Do, please, take the weight off your legs,' said Mr Davidson, drawing up a chair for Mrs Mure-Thompson.

'It's tight under my arms.' said Robert, without having to be asked.

'I thought so,' said Mrs Mure-Thompson. 'What about this one?'

'It hasn't any pockets.'

'Pockets. Yes. What,' she asked Mr Davidson, 'is a boy's coat if it doesn't have pockets? A coat without pockets is a coat for a little *person*. It is not a coat for a boy. What would he do with his hands? Where would he keep his penknife and his sweeties, Mr Davidson?' She elaborated on this subject until Mr Davidson's professional courtesy ran out of its usual willingness to comply.

'It's quite a popular coat, I assure you. And if nothing else, then at least it wouldn't bag out at the sides with the things boys keep in their pockets.'

'Baby rabbits' said Robert, whose confidence was growing.

'What?'

Mrs Mure-Thompson threw her head back and laughed with unexpected pitch. 'Yes,' she said. 'What about his baby rabbits? I'd forgotten all about *them*.'

Robert chose a green tweed coat with deerhorn buttons. It had double cuffs, shaped and hemmed in the style of jackets that are worn with kilts. It had deep pockets. It even had a deep inside pocket. 'Real tweed,' said Mr Davidson, appreciating his wares. He offered a view of the label at the back of the neck. 'Without a doubt, this is the real Mackay. And if I may say so,' he said, apologetic for raising the subject, 'it's excellent value for money.' He looked first at Mrs Mure-Thompson and then at Robert. 'Try it on again,' he said persuasively, helping Robert into its sleeves.

Mr Davidson stood back and appraised the coat with his draper's hypocrisy. He bent down and turned up the hem for Mrs Mure-Thompson to see. 'Plenty of room for growth. It wouldn't be one of these coats that'll wear for a year and then you find it's too wee for him.' Mr Davidson's head was at Robert's head height. 'It's a *lovely* coat. It's just a magnificent wee fit for the boy,' he said to Mrs Mure-Thompson as he darted to one side to examine Robert and the coat from what seemed a peculiar angle, the revelations of which were known only to drapers of Mr Davidson's experience. 'Oh, yes, it suits you! It suits you down to the ground! Mrs Mure-Thompson, you must agree!'

'Robert?'

'How much is it?' the boy asked. Mrs Mure-Thompson smiled. Mr Davidson laughed.

'It'll be a long time before you have to worry about considerations of *that* nature,' said Mr Davidson as he patted Robert on the head. 'Will I wrap it up?'

'If it's what you want, Robert?'

'Yes. Thanks very much. I like it.'

'On the account?'

'If you would, Mr Davidson.'

'Certainly.'

While they were waiting in the empty department, Mrs Mure-Thompson beckoned Robert to her chair. He consented to a brief cuddle. 'I'm glad you like that coat,' she said, 'because it's exactly the one I like best, too. Now, isn't that a happy coincidence?'

They went to the front of the shop. 'Bye-bye,' Robert said to the woman assistant, who was measuring cloth for someone else.

'Oh, cheerio, son,' she said, grateful for the unexpected civility.

Mr Davidson presented Robert with his coat tied up in a cardboard box as soon as they reached the door.

It was after five o'clock. The street was busy with traffic. Robert noticed that they walked past Mrs Mure-Thompson's car.

'We're going to the bookshop,' she explained. 'Do you like Mr Laing's shop?'

'I've never been in it.'

'Then I'm sure he'll be absolutely delighted to see you!'

Profuse welcomes met them as they went in the door. Robert's nose was tantalized by the smell of decades of paper. The books that Mrs Mure-Thompson had come to collect were already wrapped and waiting for her. Mr Laing, a thin, ascetic man with drawn cheeks and fair, bushy eyebrows, talked to Mrs Mure-Thompson about the books reviewed in the batch of clippings from newspapers and magazines which she presented to him as her new order. Robert was invited to browse. He did so against his inclination, because he had been warned not to take advantage of Mrs Mure-Thompson, who, when the mood was on her, would buy you anything you had the cheek to ask for or showed any interest in.

'Don't be shy,' she said when she joined him among the books. 'Your coat didn't turn out as expensive as I thought it might. Do, please, have them if you want.' She coaxed him with a smiling tilt of her head.

'I think my mother would be angry.'

'Ah. I see. Well, I'm sure I can smooth things over for you. What did she say to you?'

'She said she'd be angry if I came back with more than a coat.' He knew that if he said that his mother had warned him not to take advantage of Mrs Mure-Thompson, then Mrs Mure-Thompson might have cause to be angry herself, probably with both of them. Worse, she might take the coat back.

'I do so much approve of you having these books, Robert. How on earth will you be able to tell me what you think of my own little book if you haven't read these? I'm being quite selfish, you see. I'm not being kind – not in the *slightest*.'

'My mum'll skelp me.'

'No – no, she won't. I shall *speak* to her.'

She took the books to Mr Laing, who wrapped them up. Once again, money did not change hands. Mysteriously, Mrs Mure-Thompson was able to acquire what she wanted without so much as producing a purse, let alone studying the insides of one with that expression of calculating anxiety that Robert's mother adopted when they went to the shops together.

'Well, now that everything's been attended to, we'll make our way home. Shall we?' she asked, as if she were willing to go somewhere else if Robert suggested it.

They drove out of the town. The box with Robert's new coat in it lay at his feet. His three books in their brown-paper parcel sat on his lap. They passed the main gate of the airbase.

'Did you know that the officer in command there is a friend of Mr Mure-Thompson's? Well, he is. He's a very old friend of the family. And one day,' she said, 'I'll take you to see him. I know how much you like planes. Would you like that?'

'Yes.'

They slowed at the humpbacked bridge. They passed a tractor. Robert turned round to see who was driving it. 'Jack Anderson's brother,' he said. 'A horse stood on his foot last year. He had to have an injection.'

'The horse,' asked Mrs Mure-Thompson, 'or Jack Anderson's brother?'

'No. Tom Anderson.' He wondered at what she had said, and couldn't decide if it was a mistake or stupid. 'The horse?'

Mrs Mure-Thompson laughed. She turned carelessly into the B road that led to the village. 'It was a joke,' she said. 'It was just a joke.'

She must be enjoying herself, Robert thought.

When they entered the drive to the Mure-Thompson's house, Mr Mure-Thompson's car was already parked outside the front door.

'Now, isn't that just like him?' she said. 'How will I be able to put my car in the garage?'

Robert's mother was on the doorstep, with her coat and hat on. They got out of the car. Before anyone could say anything,

Mr Mure-Thompson and a guest he had brought home appeared in the garden at the side of the house, strolling and talking. They waved.

'Visitors?' Mrs Mure-Thompson asked, half excited, half disappointed.

'A gentleman from Canada, I believe.'

'Oh dear. For dinner?'

'They arrived soon after you left, Madam, so I'd time to do a nice casserole.' Mrs Duncan noticed the large, flat box that Robert held under one arm. 'And the table's all set. The soup I made earlier's more than ample for a dozen, never mind three.'

'What about dessert?' Mrs Mure-Thompson asked.

'There's the sherry trifle I made yesterday, Madam.'

'Oh, yes. Quite delicious! I think it must be Mr MacDonald, from the Toronto office,' she said, looking at the two men as they strolled across the lawn. 'Tonight,' she said to Robert, 'I shall hear all about Canada, where I've never been. Won't it be exciting?'

'I really must get on now. My man'll be famished.'

'We've had such a good afternoon, Letty. Thank you, Robert.' She looked towards the lawn and saw that her husband and his guest were walking back to the house. They gave the impression of waiting until Mrs Duncan and Robert had left before joining Mrs Mure-Thompson. She seemed to have forgotten all about the coat. 'Thank you, Letty. I honestly don't know what I'd do without you.' She seemed anxious to get rid of them. She was looking forward to something else.

Robert and his mother walked quickly down the long drive and then along the road for a bit. 'These folk'll be the death o' me, son, what wi' their unexpected guests an' dinners. He didn't so much as phone and let me know there'd be three for dinner.' They turned off into a lane. The house they lived in was at the end of it, half a mile away. On either side were high hedges, interspersed with trees. Farther on, cattle nudged up against fences on each side of the lane.

'Green,' Robert said. 'She bought me a green coat, with horn buttons.'

They stopped. 'Go on, then. Show me,' Mrs Duncan said. She began to untie the string that bound the box tight shut. 'To tell you the truth,' she said, 'I've been scared to ask what it was she bought you. If she said she was buying you a coat, you could've come home wi' very nearly anything.' Balancing the box on a raised knee, she took its lid off. 'You know, I wasn't very keen on seeing it when she was there, son.' She opened the folded tissue that lined the box. 'Oh, lovely!'

'That's what the man said.'

'What man, son?'

'Mr Davidson, in Buchanan's Drapers.'

'Buchanan's Drapers?' She took the coat from the box, laid the box on the grass, and held the coat up to look at. 'Lovely,' she said as Robert took off his school coat. He slipped into the coat that his mother held for him.

'Tweed. The real Mackay,' he said. 'That man knows what he's talking about.' He pointed to the label inside the neck of the coat. 'It says there it's real tweed. See?' he said, holding the neck open so that she could see for herself. 'And the hem.' He opened the front of the coat. 'He said I could wear it for years before it gets too wee for me.'

His mother felt the quality of the coat between her fingers. 'What's in that parcel?' she asked, noticing it for the first time.

'I couldn't help it. She said she *wanted* me to have them.'

'I told you!' She wagged her finger at him.

'I told her you'd be angry, but she said I needed them.'

'You told her I'd be angry?'

'Honest, I didn't have a chance,' he insisted. 'They were in this parcel before I could blink.'

He took the coat off, and his mother put it neatly and carefully back in its box. She smoothed the tissue, put the lid on, and tied the strings tight. She put the box under her arm. With her free hand she held Robert's hand. Robert looked at their clenched hands, because her grip was unusually firm. Under his other arm he carried his parcel of books. They walked on together.

'What in God's name will I tell your father? He'll throw a fit when he sees that coat.'

Robert had forgotten that his father would be angry. You don't get something for nothing. He had heard him say it before. 'I like it,' he said, tugging his mother's hand until she stopped in the middle of the lane, in sight of their house. 'Make him let me keep it. Please.'

FISHERMEN

Wasting my youth on the banks of Dargal Water was not a disagreeable experience. Sometimes, of course, I wish I had squandered myself in dance halls and billiard saloons, but at the time I was the same as everyone else and mad on fishing.

When I was courting my wife, Sophie, it was often along the banks of Dargal Water that we walked. She would come up from Glasgow at weekends, after we had known each other long enough for my parents not to consider that unduly progressive. We would wave to the fishermen, who would return our greetings. These were the fine summer dusks of the nineteen-fifties. Only now do I realize that my friends and neighbours, as they stood there with rod and line, or waded in quick water, expected me to return to them once I had married. Courting and study in another town signified to many of them, in their own amiable and contented ways, absence from the sport of the riverbanks.

I did not return as they expected. Instead, I settled in a city, because the parish I come from already had its dentist, who was a long way from retiring and whose dedication to rod and line made it unlikely he would move elsewhere. Fishing is now a pastime I perform on visits home, and these become rarer and rarer. There is too much to do. My wife sees the place in which I grew up as part of my memory, and therefore visits to my parents are best left to myself. 'It's better if you go by yourself,' she says. 'I'll see your parents when they come to us at Christmas. And you know how you enjoy going out to fish with your brother. You'll spend half your time in the pub, anyway, chattering to your cronies about your childhoods.'

My brother and I are not particularly close. David is a year and a half older than I, and yet, to my eyes, to my understanding, he behaves like someone several years younger. He is lean, tall, a constant and expert angler, a competitive golfer, and a bachelor of forty-two. On the other hand, I am short of stature, plump, married, with two children; and whatever perfections I once showed off with rod and line have disintegrated into the ineptitude of a man from the city. Imagining how my parents see us, as we stow our gear in the back of David's shooting brake before we drive off to the river, I admit we must look fraternal. We must look like old times – two brothers, on good terms with one another, setting off for an evening on Dargal Water. Waving to them as they see us off from the front door is for me one of these moments ripe with the unspectacular significance of our family. I would not miss the moment for anything, although I would much rather that David and I were driving straight to the Plover Inn and that for once he might give the trout a rest.

One evening, a few minutes after we had arrived, we were standing by the bank when John Henderson and Phil McGeoch turned up. They were on their way to the pub after an energetic day's fishing. 'Kenneth! Well, well – you're a stranger! How's tricks?' Henderson, who talks like that, was an inseparable of David's and mine when we were younger. He put his hand on my shoulder and looked closely at my face. 'You're looking well,' he said before he began patting me on the back as if I had swallowed something that wouldn't go down. 'Long time no see!' he said enthusiastically, shaking my hand. David looked suspicious of this passionate welcome. I was pleased to see Henderson, but I was not all that pleased. David, I imagined, was wondering if Henderson's delight would take more practical forms – namely, a suggestion that we all go to the pub immediately and have a drink for old times' sake.

'Good to see you,' said Phil McGeoch drearily. 'Still drilling holes in folks' teeth?' he asked. I had a curious feeling that there was something different about McGeoch's appearance. It was a few years since I'd come across him, but his mouth did not look the same as I remembered it. Probably my efforts to get a closer look were too professional, because McGeoch immediately bared his teeth at me in a way that made it clear he was less than pleased with a new set of dentures. 'They don't *fit* me,' he said, accusing me and all my fellow practitioners. David was amused at this riverside consultation, but he did not stop his work – lining up his tackle and picking through his boxes of flies and hooks.

'You've been allowed out late tonight,' said David.

'I've three fat trout in here,' said Henderson, patting his bag. 'That'll excuse any drinkie-winkies I get up to.'

'She's got you on a short leash?'

'Not at all,' said Henderson.

McGeoch looked up at the sound of this lie and then looked at his watch.

'All the best, Kenneth,' said Henderson, shaking my hand again. 'All the very best. And remember to pop into the Plover if you've a chance.'

'Keep up the good work,' said McGeoch, with grim sarcasm.

They disappeared along the path and were soon out of sight. 'That man McGeoch gets up my nose,' said David, passing his line coolly through the eye of a hook. 'And Henderson's wife?

Talk about punctuality? They say she charges him a fine every time he's late by so much as a minute. She chased him up the street with a bread knife. Did you hear about it? Do you know why?' David laughed as he thought about it.

'No, I haven't heard.'

'She sent him into Kilfarran to get their car resprayed.' David smirked and chuckled. 'A few days later John goes and collects it. He comes home in a blue car. 'Bronze, I said! Bronze, you fool!' She chased him up the street with the bread knife. Didn't give him a chance to explain.'

'Explain?'

'The car wasn't ready, so they loaned him another car until the bronze paint was delivered. A bread knife!'

David began walking towards a spot where his experience told him fish were likely to be. A figure called out to us, and as this was Paterson, the bank manager, David was obliged to wait until he arrived. Paterson was out of breath and puffing noisily. His face was as blotched as ever. His nose was scarlet and lumpy. He wore the same tweed hat covered in flies and hooks and was the same caricature of an angler he had always been.

'How *are* you?' He shook my hand vigorously.

'Oh, very well, Mr Paterson.'

'Ah, yes. Good. No point in complaining, is there? The financial institutions have us over a barrel,' he said confidingly. 'Lovely evening. *Lovely* evening!'

'Mrs Paterson keeping well, I hope?'

'Chirpy. Very chirpy. In the pink. Would you care for a dram?' he asked in a mischievous whisper.

'If you've got one,' I said, pretending to be surprised, which I wasn't, and looking delighted, which I was.

Paterson produced a hip flask from his fishing bag and threw off a quick drop himself before passing it to me. There was nothing in it. Not wanting to embarrass the old man, I handed it back to him, saying it was just what I needed. He passed it to

David, who struggled with what, clearly, he was pretending had been a larger gulp of the hard stuff than he had bargained for. He smacked his lips, sighed, coughed, and handed the flask back to Paterson.

'Have another,' he offered.

'No. That was fine,' I said.

'Might see you?' he asked. 'Ah, yes, I might see you later, then, in the Plover.'

'We'll be going into the Plover, won't we?'

'We might be,' said David, without looking up.

'All the very best for now, then,' said Paterson, shaking my hand once more. 'Your wife, I hope, is keeping well?'

'Oh, very well,' I said.

'Ah, yes, there will be no dental problems in your family, Kenneth.'

'Aye,' said David, 'and no money worries in yours, eh, Mr Paterson?'

The bank manager laughed. 'The benefit of a profession,' he said, 'is expert advice to oneself. Well, give my very best to your wife.'

As he walked away, we could hear his puffing and blowing when he came to the first incline on the path.

'His flask was empty,' I said as Paterson, now some way off, stopped and hoisted back an imaginary dram from his flask.

'I know.'

'You pretended.'

'You pretended as well,' said David. 'He took a cure.'

'But he was drunk. He's *usually* drunk.'

'You're out of touch.' David chuckled. 'He was kidding on. One more binge and Paterson's a corpse. Some cure, eh? He gave up everything except the action of his right hand and carrying a flask. Look, I'm getting myself over there before anyone else comes.' A few yards away he turned round and said, 'Mrs Paterson died three years ago. Or don't you remember?

And he hasn't managed the bank for five years. They sacked him. You don't seem to know anything about this place any longer.'

For a half hour I stood by myself in the gathering dusk, watching the river, and although I had a line in the water, it was entirely for the sake of keeping up appearances. David, I could see, was engaged in expert casts about two hundred yards from me. His proficiency, the deftness of his movements, even at that distance, gave me the impression that he was ahead of the fish and that he knew more about Dargal Water than they did. As a man of few words, he is suited to the solitude of angling. He looks in harmony with water and weather.

A few moments later I was startled by Bill Jamieson. He had padded up to my back in the soft shoes that he always wears without my knowing he was there until the moment when he cleared his throat. The fright of it almost made me jump in the river. Turning round to recognize him was no improvement, for I had a vague recollection of my mother saying on the telephone that Jamieson had died.

'East, west, hame's best,' he whispered, in his gruff, throaty voice. 'Now, is that not a fact, young Kenneth?'

'The fish,' I said, 'still seem a bit on the uncooperative side, even here.'

Jamieson looked disapprovingly at my preposterously dangling line. 'David,' he said, pointing to the indistinct presence of my brother, 'takes it seriously.' We looked in my brother's direction for a minute or two. The water was darker now. Noises of the stream were louder against the silence of the late dusk. The trees had shaded into dark smudges against the sky, from which the last pink and red were departing. An inevitable greyness was draining the green out of grass and leaves.

'So,' said Jamieson, 'you're back. They all come back, sooner or later. Your wife with you this time?'

'Not this time, Bill.'

'I didn't think so.'

'Too busy,' I explained, not liking the sound of his remark.

'Och, my wife's the same. Hankers after the big city. Shops and cinemas and all the rest of it. If I don't see you before you go, all the best. All the best,' he said vanishing quietly into the growing darkness on his delicately shod paws, a stealthy individual.

For another fifteen minutes I was alone. I sat down and had a smoke. Sound carries on the water at night, of course, and I could hear what I thought was David coughing farther downstream. Realizing it was someone much closer, I stood up and in the dark was bumped into by Dr Fullerton, the minister.

He peered closely at me, and as he recognized me and I recognized him, he burst out with eager greetings. We talked for a few minutes, and then I was aware of how he was standing with his feet apart, shuffling on the path, and a sound of water running into the river. A man of the cloth, I thought, ought to have had the decency to wait until he was no longer in company instead of piddling by someone's side. He sighed and readied himself for more conversation. 'My, ye probably don't know it, boy, but you were a landmark in my ministry.'

'Me?'

'Forty years've dawdled on by since I dipped your heid in the holy wash-hand basin. Now, am I right?' Dr Fullerton speaks in a homespun version of braid Scots. His humbler parishioners consider it an affectation, while the more respectable consider it a lovable eccentricity, for he comes from one of the best families of Scotland and was educated at Fettes, at the University of St Andrews, and at Balliol College, Oxford. Why he came here is a mystery. 'I never forget a baptism, and you were one o' the very furst I ever did. You might even have been the furst o' aw the babbies I've douked in the holy sink.' He thrust his feet against the ground, squaring himself up against the evening. 'Grand night. It's a *grand* night,' he said, grinding the 'r' between his teeth as if he meant to remove it from the alphabet once and for all. 'You were wedded in my kirk. My, my, birth an' weddin' an' all. An' so the grand design o' the Kirk is carried on. Your wife, Kenneth, is she well?'

'Fine an' dandy,' I said, because Dr Fullerton's idiom is catching.

'That's grand. That's *grand*,' he said, roaring with a resonance that was louder than his age should have permitted.

'Mrs Fullerton?'

'As is unfortunately well known, son, Mrs Fullerton is a first-rate pain in the neck.'

When a man is so disturbingly candid about his wife, there is little you can say in reply – at least to a minister.

'Aye,' he said, 'but it flows gently, does it not? Well, commune with it while ye've the chance, son. It never changes, but it's aye glad to see ye back, I'm sure. I'll no keep ye, then. The malt's waitin' on me doon-bye in thon Plover, an' as I always say, it's auld enough without me keepin' it waitin' any longer. God bless ye, boy.'

By then I'd had enough. Everyone, it seemed, was heading for the Plover except me. I went up the hill to the track where David had parked his shooting brake. David was soon beside me. 'This place,' he said angrily, 'is for fishing. It's a river. My permit cost me money. And it's like a street.'

'Did you catch anything?'

'Two.'

'Two what?'

'You don't even remember what folk catch in this river.'

'Oh, shut up,' I said. 'You can hardly expect me or anyone else to be as dedicated as you are.'

'That's been a wasted night. It was like listening to a wireless down there.' He slammed the rear door of the brake.

'It couldn't have been that bad. It didn't stop you catching two,' I said.

Before we got into the brake, McGeoch's eldest son and his fiancée strolled past us. 'Good evening, Mr Fraser,' he said to me. 'Good evening,' said his girlfriend.

'Oh . . . ah, good evening, Forbes.'

'Andrew,' my brother whispered.

'Good evening, Andrew,' I said, louder.

They strolled on, arm in arm.

'Get that,' I said. 'Phil McGeoch's son, and he calls me Mr Fraser. That sort of thing puts years on a man.'

'As far as he's concerned, you're just as old as his father.' He started the engine. He switched on the headlights, which cast yellow beams over the uneven track. I remembered how many times I had seen that before.

'Dad said earlier that he'd see us in the Plover.'

'Did he say if he'd drive there?' David asked.

'You don't think he'd walk it?'

'No, you're right. You'll not need me, then.'

'What?'

'Early night,' he explained. 'I've got a long weekend ahead. Golfing.'

'Right, then,' I said, disappointed. 'Suit yourself, but you can let me out at the pub.'

'What's up with you now?'

'It's a bit thick, David, standing up your own father. You know how he looks forward to having a drink with the both of us, among all that company.'

'You'll be there,' he said. 'I see Dad every day.'

'It's not often he sees us both together,' I protested.

'Whose fault is that, then?'

A few minutes later he stopped opposite the Plover. Dr Fullerton was just going in. Before the door swung shut behind him on its slow hinges, I could see my father, Jamieson,

Henderson, McGeoch, and several others I recognized. Paterson was sitting on the bench outside the pub, leaning against the wall, cured of drink and with no thirst for it, but irresistibly drawn to his damaging oasis.

'I'll be leaving early,' David said as I got out of the brake. 'So I probably won't see you in the morning.'

'Just one drink. Surely that isn't keeping you back?'

'I'm leaving at five,' he said, tapping his watch. 'And Kenneth, don't let Dad get carried away in there and drink too much. You drive back.'

David's consideration took me by surprise.

'All the best, then. I'll see you next time,' I said.

'Sure. All the very best,' he said, his hand reaching out across the passenger seat.

ORR MOUNT

Everybody knew Monty Gault. He was the local small-time builder, joiner, and handyman. No one round about the town of Dryfask thought twice about whom to get if they wanted a wall built, a floor laid, or a door hung. He could do anything connected with houses. When the Hendersons moved into Orr Mount and ran into trouble with the big contracting firm they'd hired from Glasgow, it was Monty they were advised to call for help.

'It's a funny thing,' Monty said to John Henderson, 'but I haven't seen this house up close since I was a boy.'

Orr Mount was a house about a mile west of Dryfask and 400 yards off the road, at the end of its own private lane. It was a substantial stone building in terrible disrepair, set in a garden that had surrendered to the encroachments of the woodland that hid the house from the road.

'I've been let down,' John Henderson said. 'It was two weeks ago before those fellows even made a start and did the damp courses. Now they're telling me it'll be July before they can come back.'

'You mean you accepted this estimate?' Monty whistled at the list of estimated costs that Henderson handed him and groaned at the total. 'Are you bound to this?'

'There were harsh words,' Henderson said, 'but my wife gave them the heave. Anyway, that's the estimate you've got to beat.'

'I'll work it out on paper,' Monty said, 'and let you know.'

'Could you give me a rough idea?' There was a quiet but worried urgency in Henderson's voice. 'My wife's annoyed that it's taking so long,' he said, almost confidingly. He sounded like a man who had been blamed. 'We're living in squalor.'

'I'll be cheaper,' Monty said. 'A lot cheaper. Frankly, I wouldn't have the brass neck to ask a price like that.' He slapped the estimate sheet. 'I'm a one-man band,' he went on to warn. 'I can start right away, but there's a lot to do, and it'll take time. I can do it, though. Stonework, roofing, joinery, electrics – no problem, Mr Henderson. I'll need help from time to time, but day labour's not hard to come by round here.'

Henderson was in his mid-forties – a few years older than Monty Gault, six inches taller, and greying but without distinction. He looked as much at home in his blue business suit as Monty Gault did in his faded off-brown dungarees and ancient jacket.

'It's a fine house,' Monty said, but Henderson looked at it without showing pleasure or any pride of ownership. He looked at it as though it amounted to nothing more than a drain on his bank balance and months of inconvenience until the work on it was finished.

'I didn't know the folk who lived here,' Monty said. 'I pass your road end often enough, so I used to see their car come in or out. They were the sort of people you know by their make of car. I didn't even know they'd moved,' he said. 'I thought maybe they'd changed their car. I'd forgotten it's so big a house. I hope you got it cheap, Mr Henderson.'

'At the time, I thought it was a bargain,' Henderson said. 'But yesterday the wind slammed the back door and five slates fell on the doorstep. It's been empty for over a year.'

Monty cast his eyes over the roof. He noticed a woman he took to be Henderson's wife withdraw from an upstairs window when he looked up.

'When can you start?' Henderson asked.

'As soon as you like,' Monty said. 'Don't you want a price first?'

'As long as you're a lot cheaper,' Henderson said, 'you can start tomorrow.'

At least three months of guaranteed income was a windfall that Monty Gault had not expected. Nor was it often that he had the satisfaction of renovating an entire house, he told his wife that night.

'I've a funny feeling about that job, though. There's something I don't like there.'

'Steady work,' Mary Gault said, 'and you're complaining?'

'It's Henderson. I didn't take to the man.'

'That's you all over,' Mary said. 'You're happiest when you're working for someone you like, and then it shames you to take their money.'

Quick and capable at what he did, Monty enjoyed an appreciative cup of tea with his many occasional employers. He liked his days to be neighbourly and sociable. On longer jobs, his temporary near-membership in another family gave him pleasure. He revelled in their talk and gossip; he was often delighted by the eccentric routines of different households, moved by their sadnesses, and dispirited by their tensions. Orr Mount and its occupants were outside the circle of shared local personality and behaviour – they were tucked away from the life of the district – and Monty was unsure what he'd find there.

The following morning, Monty parked his van behind Orr Mount, curious to meet Mrs Henderson for the first time.

She greeted him at the back door. 'You know, of course, that we were let down?'

If anything, Mrs Henderson looked more on edge than her husband. There was a depressed kind of determination about her that Monty thought might be a response to the discomfort of her surroundings. The kitchen would have been modern in 1920; its obsolescence had brought a heavy, dark shabbiness. Everything in the room was makeshift, and utensils were still mostly packed in tea chests and cardboard boxes. 'It's filthy,' she told Monty. 'How could people live in dirt like this?' She glanced around her with disgust. 'I want you to start with the window frames.'

'Window frames first?' Monty asked. His ordering of priorities was different. He had come prepared, he told her, to make a start on the roof, some of which had grown a green patina. Here and there on its slipped slates there were distinct patches of moss. A sycamore sapling had taken root in the guttering. 'Then, after the downspouts, and a bit of pointing, I thought the rewiring, Mrs Henderson, followed by an all-out assault on this mess in here. The kitchen speaks for itself,' he said.

But she was firm. 'You don't have to live with the draughts in this house. No, the window frames. They rattle every time there's a puff of wind. *Then* the roof. But we'll see about that once you've shown me what you can do. You *can* make window frames?' she asked sternly.

'Oh, I've made a few in my time,' Monty said, trying to laugh off his surprise at her question and her manner – both of which insisted that Mrs Henderson would stand for no nonsense. 'I take it you're the boss,' he said. 'I like to know who I'm working for.'

'No, you're working for Mr Henderson,' she said.

But Monty was unconvinced. Why, he asked himself, do some wives pretend that their husbands are the masters of the household when it's as clear as day that they aren't? He had seen the relationship many times before. It was one of the facts of life that kept him in work: wives nagging their menfolk to fix things around the house, and then – when it dawned on them that their husbands wouldn't, or couldn't, do the work themselves – urging them to get Monty Gault in to do it.

'Well, I like my hot cups, Mrs Henderson,' he said. 'I'm an old-fashioned tradesman. I'll work better for a steady flow – tea or coffee, but tea's preferred, a touch of milk and no sugar.'

He spent the morning measuring the windows. Through the glass he observed in passing much of the work ahead. Floors dipped visibly where the joists were rotten. Naked light bulbs hung on the ends of old braided electric wire. Damp patches greyed through paint and paper on walls and ceilings. At each symptom of neglected husbandry, Monty winced in consternation.

He was on a ladder finishing with the upper windows when he looked into a room and saw a child in bed with bandaged eyes. Gauze and bedding obscured most of the child's face, and Monty could not tell if it was a boy or girl. Apart from the child's bed, a chair, and a small table, the room was raw and unfurnished. Monty stood frozen on his ladder and, through his slow shock, tried to understand what he saw. He checked over his measuring, and came down to find Mrs Henderson.

'I was frightened I'd wake him up.' He felt he should have been warned. 'A noise at the window, and him with his eyes bandaged – that'd scare anybody. Did he have an accident?'

'He's blind,' she said. 'They tried an operation on his right eye. They did something to the other eye, too. I should've told you he was up there.' She poured tea for Monty. 'He's been at home with us for the past week. We couldn't postpone the operation – a thing like that can't be put off because a builder drags his heels and lets you down. And we couldn't stay on in our old house. We'd sold it, and the buyers needed to move in. We were tied to a date. Robin's thirteen. I knew the operation would be a waste of time.'

'Has he always been blind?' Monty asked solicitously.

'No, not always.' Her tone made it clear she did not want to talk about her son. 'I know exactly what I have in mind for this house,' she said. But having changed the subject, she said, 'You're probably wondering why we took the place, with all its problems.'

'It's none of my business,' Monty said. 'I'm just the hired help.'

'Good,' she said. 'I'm glad you know where we stand. It's difficult enough as it is without tradesmen carrying tales about us.'

'You weren't keen on me doing the work here, were you?' Monty asked.

'You're a bit too local.'

'Am I fired?'

'Robin will be much nearer a very good school for the blind. In fact, he's been a pupil there for almost a year. Living here saves me forty miles' driving a day. How long will the window frames take?'

'I don't know,' Monty said. 'A week to make, maybe more. And a week to set them in. Give or take a few days,' he said.

'I want replicas of the original windows. Exact copies, and the best materials.'

'His eyes were bandaged,' Monty told his wife that night. 'Great wads of gauze and surgical tape. Sound asleep. He didn't move a muscle. I was really shaken.'

'You always take other people's troubles too much to heart,' Mary said. 'That'll be why you've been hard at it out there until the back of eight.'

'There's a lot of window frames,' he protested. 'It'll be twelve hours a day until it's done.'

'Make it last,' Mary said. 'We need the money.'

* * *

Protected by plastic sheeting and tarpaulin, glazed, neatly primed and undercoated, the window frames arrived at Orr Mount on Saturday morning.

'I was wondering where you were! I was getting ready to come and find you,' Henderson said. His tone was more irate than he could quite bring off.

'What's wrong?' Monty asked.

'Where've you been?' Henderson said.

'Me? Where'd you think? I've been in my yard, busy making your window frames.' Monty opened the back of the van.

'That surely isn't all of them?' Henderson said truculently.

'It's a wee van,' Monty said, pointing out the obvious. 'I'll have to go back for the rest of them.' In the past, he had endured inspections of his work by half-wits and incompetents, but Henderson's insinuation of indolence, or dishonesty, or the one excusing the other, was new to him. It rattled Monty. He turned round and saw Mrs Henderson approaching. Monty said to her, 'I'm sorry, Mrs Henderson. I thought you understood I'd have to get the wood milled and then make up the window frames on my bench. That's the sort of job I do in the yard.'

'I phoned,' she said. 'Three times I phoned you.'

'The phone's in the house,' Monty said, 'and Mrs Gault goes out to work.'

'I hope the wood is properly seasoned,' she said to her husband.

'Is it?' Henderson asked, passing on the suspicion.

Monty pulled a window frame free of its wadding. He was losing patience. 'Tap that,' he said sharply. 'Go on, tap it.' Henderson rapped on the wood. 'Should they bend, buckle, or rot, you know where to come. Now, is that a perfect copy of that window over there, or is it not?'

Mrs Henderson began counting them. 'Where are the rest?'

'Maybe I could have got them all into the van, Mrs Henderson, by squeezing them in, and scratching the undercoats, and risking a lot of broken glass on that bumpy joke you call a road. Now, I think the three of us ought to have a wee talk. There's someone round here thinks I've been swinging the lead, and I don't like it.'

Mrs Henderson walked away and left her husband to apologize.

'We hadn't seen hide or hair of you the whole week,' Henderson said, venturing an explanation for his previous ill temper. His right leg trembled, his heel throbbing on the matted grass.

'I could see you were in a bad mood when you came back to collect the second batch of frames,' Mary Gault told Monty later. 'I suppose you just stood there and took it?'

'I did not,' Monty said. 'I gave them a piece of my mind.'

'Tipped your forelock and said 'Sorry,' if I know you,' Mary said. 'They want you on the cheap. I expect they've made you think they're doing you a favour. Did they pay you?'

'Monday,' Monty said.

'Eight or nine o'clock every night this week, and you have to wait until Monday?'

Monty spent the following week installing the window frames. 'They make a difference,' he said to Henderson, who pretended unsuccessfully to show an interest.

'It wasn't easy,' Monty went on. 'I hope you don't think that the man I brought in to lend a hand was a matter of handouts to my pals. I needed him for the upstairs windows. How's your son, Mr Henderson?'

'They're taking the bandages off in a few days.' Henderson sighed. 'Hospitals.'

Monty said, 'I can well understand how you haven't much heart for the work that's on hand here.'

'I feel bad about putting a boy through an operation like that,' Henderson said. 'All that hope, for nothing.'

'Still, you did it for the best,' Monty said. 'Well, once I've got these frames painted, I think the roof's next.'

'You'll have to ask my wife,' Henderson said. 'She's got it all worked out.'

'You might try putting your hand to the garden,' Monty said. It sounded like homely, rural advice. 'It could help take your mind off things.' Henderson's look made Monty feel that either he had said the wrong thing or Henderson's troubles were inconsolable.

Before he went home that evening Monty walked over the front garden, searching for an impression of what it must have been like under a conscientious owner. Weeds and wildness blended into the woodland at the garden's edge. Posts of a rotten fence were swamped by billows of runaway roses. An invasive bramblebrake, its briars and tendrils freshly green, crept towards unpruned shrubs. Daffodils and narcissi survived and bloomed here and there in the rampant neglect.

'You've a big job ahead of you here,' Monty said to Mrs Henderson, who had come out to him from the house. 'Have you any plans for it?'

'First things first,' she said. She looked around her with loathing. She picked up a forgotten rusted trowel from where it lay embedded in the grass and threw it into the brambles. 'Ugh,' she said.

While Monty painted the window frames at the back of the house, Mrs Henderson painted those on the ground floor at the front. He was disappointed; he had hoped for her conversation. He went round to see how she was doing.

She wore a head scarf. Her hands were spotted with paint and a small smear marked her face.

'Oh dear,' Monty said, noticing that her green sweater had recently touched wet white paint somewhere. 'There's the spot,' he said, pointing to the sill, where wrinkled paint was furred with strands of wool. 'No, don't touch it. Wait until the frame dries, then sand it down lightly and then repaint it. Apart from that, you're doing fine.'

After a moment, he went on. 'I saw your boy reading a book in Braille in there. That's wonderful. He showed me a bit about how it works. God forbid I should go blind, but if I did I ask myself if I could master that.'

'Shouldn't you be working?' she asked.

'Tea break,' he said. 'Mind you, I expect no tea right now, but it's time.'

'Am I taking the bread out of your mouth by doing this?' she asked.

'Would it make any difference if I said you were?'

'Robin's all right by himself, you know,' Mrs Henderson said. 'He likes reading. He manages better than you think. Manages us, too.'

When the windows were finished, Monty worked on the roof. He cut out and replaced rotted timbers, renewed slates, rebuilt the chimney stacks. He was hanging new gutters one afternoon when a car drew up at the back of Orr Mount and a woman got out. The mossed and weedy gravel was not to her liking; she seemed to set her feet down carefully as she walked round to the other side of the car. The passenger, a girl Robin's age, had already stepped out and stood waiting. She took the woman's arm, and they crossed the runnelled surface together, the woman warning the girl when they approached tufts of long grass near the back door of Orr Mount. The woman looked up, and Monty waved to her. She smiled halfheartedly. Monty suspected he had been too familiar.

Not long after they had gone inside, Monty heard a piano being played. The music went on for over an hour. The tunes were familiar, yet somehow the piano sound seemed unusual.

'It never crossed my mind that it was the two of them playing at once,' Monty said to Mrs Henderson when the guests had left and he went in for his tea. 'At first I thought it might be the wireless.'

'They're not prodigies, you know,' she replied. 'A lot of blind children learn to play the piano.'

'Well, I think it's marvellous. It had a nice swing to it.'

Mrs Henderson did not share his enthusiasm. 'Four hands thundering away at a pop song isn't my idea of music,' she said. 'They're taught to play at school – that was one of the reasons we wanted Robin to go there. I know he plays Mozart and Chopin for his teacher, because I've heard him. But at home all he wants to play is these awful songs he picks up from the radio. Are you musical?'

'No, but I can dance,' Monty said. 'To play music for dancing is a wonderful thing to be able to do. It's like being able to make people laugh, if you know what I mean.'

'Dancing's changed a lot since my day,' she said.

'I'm fifteen years out of date,' Monty said. 'So, thank God, is everyone else in Dryfask – at least of my generation. We have dances at the community hall once a month. You should ask Mr Henderson to take you. You'd enjoy it – everyone's very friendly.'

'I don't think so,' said Mrs Henderson. 'When you're finished outside, I want you to start on the fireplaces.'

'What about the rewiring?'

'No,' she said. 'The fireplaces.'

A look at each room challenged him with how much work he still had to get through. Cardboard boxes stood on the floors among the dust-sheeted furniture in the front rooms, where Mrs Henderson had already begun stripping wallpaper. Monty watched Robin help her by pulling at a loose flap. The boy looked up with his sightless eyes as he tugged at the layered wallpaper, which peeled vertically and then rose in a drizzle of old plaster.

At home, Monty told his wife, 'She watches me make good the stone and brickwork in those fireplaces as if she's dying to have a go at that, too! It wouldn't surprise me if she could do it. Talk about organized, Mary! She's got a whole list of what needs doing, at least six pages long, and she's very firm about how she wants it done.'

'And that sticks in your craw,' Mary said. 'You who like to be your own boss.'

'I don't understand it. Those old marble mantelpieces were lovely, but she's had me rip them out. 'Careful,' she says. 'I've sold them to an antique dealer.' Old jobs out, and what comes in instead? Older ones! But very nice, Mary. Beautiful old wooden fireplaces, stripped down to the timber, and she says she'll polish them herself. I'll say this for Mrs Henderson. The woman's got taste.'

'She can afford it,' Mary said.

'I dare say,' Monty said. 'Henderson's a civil servant, but he must be pretty high up. Still, if they were that rich, they wouldn't have come down the market and asked Monty Gault to work for them.'

Henderson came home one late afternoon while Robin and the young girl, Gillian, were playing a tune Monty had asked them for. He found Monty humming along as he screwed in a new wall socket.

'Do you think she's asking for too many outlets?' Henderson said.

'If there's one thing I've learned,' Monty said, 'it's to do what your wife tells me. She's a very practical woman, and she's nearly always right.' He consulted his diagram. 'Now, if I've got this wrong there'll be an almighty bang that'll blow the fuse box off the wall and through the roof.'

Monty's exaggeration drew Henderson to glance at the diagram, but he pulled back in incomprehension. He looked uneasily at a rugged channel gouged up the wall to lead the wires to the floor above. It looked like a ghastly, irreparable error.

'Personally,' Henderson said, 'I felt we should've got a proper electrician to do this.'

Monty frowned at him. 'I thought those days were over,' he said curtly but confidently, making his remark sound one of sorrow rather than anger.

'As long as you're sure,' Henderson said.

Monty lay down to winkle a wire under the floorboards. 'I know a man who'd do that garden for you,' he said. From his prone position, he saw Henderson's leg tremble and his heel beat on the floor at twice the tempo of the tune from the piano. Monty got up and roughly began prising a floorboard loose with a crowbar. Nails sprang free, and the board split.

'Rotten timbers,' he said. 'They were ready for the bonfire anyway. This man I know could go through that jungle in no time. Shall I ask him?'

'No,' Henderson said. 'The garden's my responsibility. I'll get round to it.'

'Suit yourself,' Monty said. 'It was just an idea.'

'I wish they'd play something else,' Henderson said. 'Four hands on a piano just rams home the mistakes. It gets on my nerves.'

'I like it,' Monty said. 'They're playing it for me. Your boy's as bright as a button, and he and Gillian make a good team.'

'They're very close,' Henderson said impulsively. 'We find it worrying. Gillian's his only friend, you see. And she's as blind as he is.'

Puzzled, Monty put his weight on the crowbar, and another floorboard creaked upward with a *ping* of nails and the destructive noise of wood tearing. 'But the two of them get on fine,' he said.

'Of course, we can't really discourage them,' Henderson said. 'It's just a bit upsetting that they're so inseparable. The Hepburns feel the same about Gillian. When you're bringing up a child who's blind, you're thinking about the future all the time. It's not easy for a boy like Robin to make friends with sighted children.'

Rich summer growth made more conspicuous than ever the tumbling, nettled, indiscriminate verdure of the garden at Orr Mount. Monty was dismayed. In Dryfask, unkempt gardens and shabby houses were taken as signs of the demoralization of their owners – symptoms of what was known locally as 'falling out with yourself'. Two months of mild evenings had passed, he reflected, in which Henderson could have made a start against the years of neglect. Nor had he laid a hand on the house.

'Paint-stripping coming on well, I see,' Monty said to Henderson, in the sly hope of shaming him. 'Slowly but surely. It's a heartbreaking job your wife's taken on there.' Days and days of Mrs Henderson's fastidious work with a scraping knife and a noxious-smelling chemical had turned out to be in vain, for the bottom inch of the skirting-boards on the ground floor was revealed to be damp and rotten under the layers of paint and varnish. It was like watching an archaeologist.

'But we're getting there,' Henderson said.

'There's light at the end of the tunnel.'

'As they say, it's very often the lamp on an oncoming train,' Monty said.

Henderson's worried uselessness bothered Monty. It was bred into Monty's bones that a man should neither be so lazy nor feel himself so superior as to shy away from turning a hand on his own property. Still, he thought,

> It is the business of the wealthy man
> To give employment to the artisan.

Work was getting harder to find. The longer the Orr Mount renovations lasted, the better it was for him. He hoped, too, that his performance in these substantial repairs might lead Henderson to offer him the lighter job of painting and decorating.

But when Monty saw Mrs Henderson tackle the tousled and thorny wilderness around Orr Mount he felt guilty at hoping for more work through Henderson's laziness or ineptitude. Mrs Henderson stooped down and snipped savagely at the rugged grass with a pair of garden shears. Monty turned away from the window with contempt for her husband's handlessness. The click of the shears slowed and then jammed altogether on a resistant divot. He could imagine the strain in the woman's arms, the impossible task of driving through those matted tufts with mere heavy-duty shears. What was called for was a strong man with a scythe, or something mechanical. Better still, the lumpy, repulsive meadow that the lawn had become ought to be dug up and re-turfed.

Monty continued with his plastering, expecting at any moment to witness Mrs Henderson give up in despair. But each time he looked out of the window she was shearing as vigorously as ever, and getting nowhere. He watched as her elbows shot up at each side with the action of her gigantic scissoring. Her arched back rose and fell with the effort.

After almost an hour, Monty could bear it no longer, and he went out to her. 'Honest, Mrs Henderson, if you want to do that, you should get the right tools for the job.' Smeared with wet grass and mud, the blades of her shears ripped viciously at a heavy tuft. 'You'll be at it this time next year,' he said, trying to make a joke of it. 'You'd as well gnaw at it with your teeth as pluck and pull with that. You'll never do it.'

She turned round and looked up at him. Her face was flushed with effort, and the strain of her labour, and her thoughts had made her face hard-favoured and bitter. Her cheeks ran with tears. She stood up breathlessly, wiped her face on her sleeve, and threw the shears to the ground.

'Many's the man who'd look at that mess and run a mile before he'd work a spade on it,' Monty said. 'Mrs Henderson, there's a pal of mine who'd transform it in a week. It'd save you both a lot of trouble.' His tone suggested he understood that the garden controversy expressed some profound matrimonial obstacle between the Hendersons. 'Would you like me to ask him to come by?'

'No, I would *not*!' she said angrily. 'How dare you interfere? I know who'll do this garden, and it won't be your friend.'

It was clear that Mrs Henderson's anger and her tears were not those of weakness or self-pity but of determination. Embarrassed and apologetic, Monty knew better than try to console her. When she walked away, he left it at that and went back to work.

Nor did he mention Mrs Henderson's tearful and violent gardening to Mary. Still, he couldn't help complaining to her about Henderson. 'He's spending money hand over fist on the house, I'm working miracles inside, and outdoors it's like an Amazonian nature reserve. God knows what wild beasts are roaming through that undergrowth.'

'I don't see why they don't get a man to do the garden,' Mary said.

'Actually,' Monty said, 'if I got the painting and decorating I wouldn't mind doing the garden myself. It'd finish the work nicely. I'd get a real kick out of that.'

'I don't care what you do,' Mary said, 'so long as it means steady money. I'm getting used to being able to pay the bills.'

'I'd like your advice,' Henderson said to Monty a few weeks later. The contracted work was nearly done. 'I want the kitchen floor laid with quarry tiles. Can you recommend a reliable tiler?'

'How about me?'

'Can you? Surely you haven't had much experience of tiling?'

'Have I let you down yet?'

'To tell you the truth,' Henderson said, 'I'm looking for someone to do the decorating.' It sounded close to the offer Monty had hoped for, but he waited to be asked directly. 'I told Mrs Henderson I wasn't sure if it was quite your line of country.'

'Are you asking me?' Monty said.

'It's too much for us to manage on our own, what with me at work . . .' Henderson said lamely.

'I can do it,' Monty said.

Mrs Henderson's excitement and satisfaction at the progress made on her house, and the faint sound of the piano downstairs when Robin was allowed to play, made Orr Mount a happier house than Monty had known it. It was as if the incident in the garden had never happened, that animal clack of shears and furious tearing of grass. There was no forgetting it, though, or the fact of the garden, with its vegetation as energetic as ever. Very soon, Monty thought, the Hendersons would be sleeping in a bedroom that was in mint condition. But when they got up in the morning and drew the curtains, the lively, wicked overgrowth – all that strangled greenery, dripping with dew – would stare at them in challenge.

Henderson, too, was in a better frame of mind. He came home early one day. 'I collected the curtains,' he said proudly.

Monty helped him unload, and Mrs Henderson set off towards the back door with her arms laden with fabric. 'Where did you put the rods?' he asked Henderson.

'I couldn't get them into the car,' Henderson said, apparently unaware of the importance of his omission. 'They're long things.'

'Your wife'll be furious! She's dying to get these up. The rods are plastic – you could've bent them.'

'Some of them are wooden poles,' Henderson said stubbornly.

'We could've done without the poles, for the moment – they're for the sitting room. But we need the rods *now*.' Monty was openly exasperated. 'Look, I'll go and get them. Where's the receipt?'

Henderson fished a piece of paper from his wallet in silence. He was clearly offended at Monty's tone as he went on. 'You've got a roof rack there, Mr Henderson. You could've tied the rods on to that if you didn't want to bend them. You don't think!' Monty got into his van, leaving Henderson expostulating quietly.

When Monty got back with the rods an hour later, Mrs Henderson was cooking dinner.

'I know it's late,' she said, 'but do you think you could put these up in the bedroom?' It was a cold and formal request, without a hint of thanks in her voice.

'Never mind,' he said to himself as he sat on the window ledge upstairs, forcing the hooks through slots in the curtain tape. 'So long as we keep the peace.'

It was already dark when he got into his van. He looked up and saw Mrs Henderson pulling the curtains shut, then opening and closing them again. She did this several times. It was now a better window than the one at which he had first seen her, he reflected.

Sitting down to his own dinner, Monty told Mary, 'I know I'm far from perfect –'

'You can say that again. What time do you call this to come home, without so much as giving me a ring to warn me?'

'– but you wouldn't last ten minutes with that man Henderson. Now, there's an imperfect man for you,' Monty said.

'At least,' Mary said, 'he's got money, and he gets home at a decent hour.'

'The story of my life,' Monty said. 'I oblige folk by staying a bit later to get a job finished, and when I get back here I'm nagged for it. Mary, I'm a handyman. It's my business to be obliging. Will you never understand that?'

When it came the turn of the sitting room at Orr Mount, Mrs Henderson helped Monty move the furniture into the hall – everything except the piano. 'No, it's too heavy to move,' she said. 'It would block the hall. Leave it in the middle and cover it with a tarpaulin. Frankly,' she said, 'I'd as soon see the back of it.'

Monty glanced at her in surprise, but she was looking elsewhere. 'It takes up a lot of room in this house, one way and another,' she said.

It was near the end of the school holidays. Robin sat in his room upstairs or at the kitchen table, where he read, his fingers feeling over the sheets of text, his head turned thoughtfully to one side.

The boy missed playing his piano. His mother was in town ordering furniture, and he came into the sitting room where Monty stood on a stepladder, painting the cornices in deep concentration. Robin reached under the tarpaulin and played a loud chord.

'You gave me a fright, Robin!' Monty cried.

'Will you be finished in this room soon?' the boy asked.

'Give it three or four days,' Monty said. 'I'll be as quick as I can. I miss the sound of your music. But your mother told you to stay in the kitchen. If she catches you in here, there'll be trouble.'

Robin ran his fingers over the keyboard. 'Do you know where the wireless is?' he asked.

'Isn't it in the kitchen?'

'I can't find it,' the boy said.

'Come and I'll help you look for it.' Monty climbed down and put his hand on Robin's shoulder, meaning to guide him, but the boy led the way.

The radio was on a shelf too high up for Robin to have reached. Monty wondered why Mrs Henderson had put it up there when she knew that Robin liked to listen to it.

'Where was it?' Robin asked.

'It was on the chest in a corner,' Monty said, hoping to deceive him. 'There were things in front of it.'

'What things?'

'Cornflakes, washing powder,' Monty said, improvising an answer from packets he saw elsewhere in the kitchen.

Robin walked across the kitchen and put his hand on the packet of cornflakes. He lifted the packet and shook it. 'You reached up,' Robin said. 'Was it up there?'

'Are you supposed to be studying?' Monty asked.

'She hid it. She didn't want me to find it,' he said.

'Then if your mother doesn't want you to have the wireless, maybe I shouldn't give it to you. She must have a reason,' Monty said.

'You can say you didn't know I wasn't to have it,' Robin said.

A new bathroom was installed, and Monty's last job was tiling and painting it.

'Unless we've missed something,' he said to Mrs Henderson as he washed, 'I think that's it.'

They walked into the sitting room and she gave him a glass of sherry. 'I won't sit down in these overalls,' Monty said, conscious also of his working shoes on the Persian rug. He put his glass down and stepped off the carpet, kneeling to run his hand over the mellow glow he had succeeded in bringing out on the old parquet floor. 'I knew this floor had life left in it,' he said. 'It's come up a treat. It must have been hidden under those old carpets and underlays for years, just waiting for someone like you, Mrs Henderson – an appreciative owner who'll take good care of it.'

'There are one or two lumpy bits,' Mrs Henderson said. 'Otherwise I'm very pleased with it.'

Pictures now hung on the sitting-room walls. Rugs and chintzes brought a bright, complacent richness to the large room. There were books in the bookcases, and ornaments had come forth from the tea chests and boxes that had once littered the unkempt interior.

'This room has class,' Monty said. 'I like it. It has taste.' He waved his arm in a survey of the sitting room. 'I've done the heavy work, but I can see now what you had in mind all along. I must say, though, that it's a pity, a great pity, about the garden.' He smiled cautiously. 'I don't want to interfere, Mrs Henderson, but I've a living to earn. I'm making you an offer.'

Robin ran into the room, leading Gillian by the hand. 'My mother will be back for me at five. Is it all right?' Gillian said.

Eagerly, Robin asked, 'May we please play the piano for a bit?'

'No, you may not,' Mrs Henderson said. 'I'm speaking to Mr Gault.'

'Don't stop them on my account,' Monty said.

'Please, Mummy!' Robin said, put out by the delay.

'Go ahead then!' Mrs Henderson said angrily. She turned back to Monty. 'You *are* interfering,' she told him quietly. 'I'm sure you mean well, but the garden's not for you to do. No longer than fifteen minutes!' she shouted crossly to Robin, who made no acknowledgement. 'Did you hear me? Robin! Fifteen minutes and no more!'

'I'm sorry,' Monty said. 'I knew it rankled, but I thought maybe I'd be helping you out. And helping me out, too,' he added. 'I don't deny it.'

'I'll send my husband over with the money he owes you,' she said.

'It's not for me to talk about what's wrong here,' he said. 'But you're not trying, Mrs Henderson, and neither's he. You're making a big mistake. I wish you all joy of your house. Take care of it. There's twenty years of my hard-earned experience in the work I've put into it. And it would've pleased *me* to see it finished.'

Four young hands ventured on the first bars of a tune. As Monty left the house, he heard Mrs Henderson shout, 'Will you shut up that racket!'

Driving off, Monty saw Henderson's car approaching his own van on the narrow lane that led to the Dryfask road. He stopped in the middle of the lane, so that Henderson had to stop, too. He got out of the van and walked to Henderson's lowered window.

'You've the swankiest house in Dryfask, and the nastiest garden I ever saw. That won't be gardening; it'll be pioneering. You've got pixies in your orchard!' he shouted, exasperated, as Henderson stared at him incredulously. 'Do yourself a favour, Henderson. Get it done, and fast! Get it done before it's too late!' He started to return to his van but stopped and went back to Henderson. 'I'm talking about your garden. Can you wield a scythe? You'll have to learn!'

Henderson leaned on his horn. It was an angry, demented noise that howled over the countryside. Once back in his van, Monty Gault retaliated, and pressed on his. Their vehicles were almost nose to nose before Monty swerved and pulled up beside Henderson. 'If you need me,' he shouted, 'you know where to find me!'

BOYFRIENDS AND GIRLFRIENDS

Kemshill Community Association organized 'social evenings' for every second Saturday during the winter months. Couples were encouraged to bring their children – a gesture that was unpopular with some but welcomed by most, especially by teenage girls still too young to be allowed to travel to dance halls; they looked after the children between 6.30 and 7.30, when whist, which bored them, was played. Nine o'clock was a late hour for children to stay up in those days, the late 1940s. Postwar social change, an earnest gaiety, a sober optimism filtered through to places like Kemshill – places that are minor, perhaps, but where more of the world lives than the headlines and passions of history would have us believe.

A drummer, an accordionist and a saxophonist struck up music for dancing after the tables and chairs had been cleared to the sides of the hall. Mr Hogg, who organized these evenings, sprinkled rosin on the floor to give the dancers a footing. For us children this provided the best fun of all: no one minded when, a sausage roll in one hand and a cake in the other, we tested the floor with sliding. Known as 'the purvey', the sausage rolls and cakes lay on long wooden baker's trays on a trellis table at one end of the hall, beside the tea urns and a crate of lemonade bottles.

We would sit at the side, listening to the band, watching our parents dance to 'Heartaches', 'I'll Never Smile Again', 'Fascination'. Sometimes, without actually asking, Dorothy Gordon made it plain that she wanted me to dance with her. That ten-year-old couple made a mess of it. I was all heels, knees, and elbows, and so was Dot Gordon, except that she was too proud to admit it.

Dot's mother was a war widow, a melancholy, short-tempered woman with dark hair. One Saturday night she burst into tears during a slow dance in the arms of Ralph Harvie, who had known her husband. For a moment, it did not surprise me; many of the tunes that our parents hummed or sang as they smiled and stepped around the hall sounded very sad. Their cadences probed wordlessly into a life of which I knew nothing. (Either that or the trio on the platform were miserable.) Yet just as often the sadness was dispelled: 'Deep Purple' and 'Remember Me' gave way to 'Puttin' on the Ritz' or Scottish dances. At the sound, the old wifies gathered by the tea urns perked up and trotted to the floor, calling on elderly husbands, who knew these dances and no others.

But maybe it wasn't the music that made Dot's mother cry. Ralph Harvie must have said something to her; they were talking and she ended up in tears. Women led her off the floor, and one of them threw an accusing glance at Ralph, who smiled with cautious embarrassment. My father was among the men who sat down with him. Ralph seemed to be explaining himself, and my father patted him on the back with a kind, sympathetic smile, much like the one he wore when he told Bert Nelson how sorry he was to hear about his mother.

Pity, concern, subdued anger and disguised anxiety – the whispers around the hall were unmistakably troubled. Even at my age, some native sense told me that something was going on, but that juvenile curiosity would be met with a reprimand or a lie. Dot looked worried, but she was put out, too; she resented the concern that was directed at her. No one was dancing. The musicians were talking among themselves. Mr Hogg beckoned urgently to them; I heard him say, 'Play something foot-tapping, for God's sake! You're being paid to cheer us up!'

Irene Gordon was a tragedy of the place. History and change intruded on Kemshill as much as anywhere else, if, perhaps, a little later, and they were as readily accepted, criticized, or rejected, or all three at once; but Irene Gordon, with her prestige as the only woman in Kemshill widowed by the Second World War – her daughter the only child made fatherless – was Kemshill's measure of great events. She was a statistic of sorrow; she was a favoured citizen. Women whose own men had also been in uniform must have looked at her and thought, there but for the grace of God. She was Kemshill's casualty.

Without going so far as to wear her Sunday best, Mrs Gordon would smarten herself up when she went to the post office to collect her widow's pension. Her usual style was one of principled shabbiness, so it was noticed when she did up her hair, put on a hat or a head scarf, and left her customary dilapidation behind for an hour or two. The post office was little more than a hut almost a mile from Kemshill, half-way to Overrigg and next to the railway station that in those days served both villages and now serves neither.

During school holidays, we children often played on a hill that overlooked the Overrigg road. Sometimes we saw Mrs Gordon walking along the narrow pavement. When Dot spotted her mother, she used to leave us and run down the sloping field, shouting and waving. For all her calling, Dot had usually reached the hedge by the roadside before Irene Gordon noticed her.

'I could brain that man Harvie,' I heard my mother tell my father. 'He pesters poor Irene Gordon, and it's not just when he tries to dance her on a Saturday night. Some of the men round here ought to have a word with him.' My father scowled, but she went on. 'She doesn't want him. Why can't he take no for an answer?'

'I've heard of nothing that could be held against Ralph,' my father said.

'You have now, because I've told you.'

'Irene could do worse – a lot worse. The only woman he ever wanted, and she shuts herself up in the past! It's six years since Lawrie Gordon died!'

For almost a year, there was a probationary armistice between Dot's mother and Ralph Harvie. In the spring, she let him look after her badly neglected garden. So far, convention had prevented a local man from volunteering to rehabilitate the unruly place. A brother would have been appropriate, but Irene had none; of her two brothers-in-law, one – married to her sister – lived in Glasgow and did what he could on their several yearly visits, but he knew nothing about gardens. Her dead husband's brother lived nearby in Overrigg, but he never showed his face, and was disparaged in Kemshill as a man who failed in his responsibilities towards kin. A hand from a married friend of the deceased would have been respectable, as long as his wife visited the widow while her husband forked and spaded. But Ralph Harvie was an unmarried man, whose fond designs on Irene were common knowledge; when Irene allowed him to trim the high privet hedge in front of her house, the town took it as a sign of his progress with her. It became the occasion for benign gossip.

Ralph transformed the garden. He took the squeak out of Dot's swing and oiled every hinge on the premises. He painted the gate, repaired the fence, and planted the earth in anticipation of a harvest.

Ralph was a tall, slow, good-natured and pleasant man in his thirties. He had big grey-green eyes and enormous hands. 'Ralph's onions are usually so-so,' my father once said, 'but he grows the best leeks in the village. He keeps his mother's table well provided.' Like many men in Kemshill, my father associated gardening with decency. 'Hitler was no gardener. I'll tell you that for nothing. That's a *fact*.'

For all the conversations that people in Kemshill exchanged on the subject of Ralph's wooing, Ralph Harvie and Irene Gordon said little to each other. I played in the Gordons' garden almost every day – Dot was my best friend – so I had some picture of things there. Mrs Gordon would make tea for Ralph and bring it outside in a white enamel mug, but they seldom spoke, and when they did it was not for long, or about anything but the garden. Ralph never entered the house while I was there. If he did at any other time, I'd judge he would have knocked first on the door and then gone no farther than the kitchen. She used to place the tea mug on the doorstep outside the kitchen, and they'd exchange their few words there. Ralph Harvie scraped what was left of the worn and blistered paint from the three stone steps; fresh white paint took its place – broad parallel stripes on either side of the hollowed treads. At the time I thought it insignificant, the work he devoted to those steps, but now I don't.

My mother admitted that she might have been wrong about Ralph. 'It's a big step for a woman to take. But maybe it'll be a while longer before Irene's ready.'

'They haven't been out together,' my father remarked. 'Suggest to Irene that you'd look after the girl if she and Ralph wanted to go to the pictures.'

My mother looked askance at my father in his role as go-between. Whatever might be said in my father's favour – many things – as a romancer he was a die-hard Presbyterian.

* * *

Dot Gordon had fair hair and skin so light it seemed you could see the blood through it. Eager, energetic, nimble, she could make the crossover from girls' games to tree-climbing and apple-raiding with a naturalness that made the vigour of other tomboys look forced by comparison. Most of the girls around Dot's age did not like her, perhaps because she shunned the leadership they extended to her as her right. Boys distrusted her: she ran too fast, climbed with sure feet, and refused to admire bravado or take second place.

Once, when she and I were playing together at the hump-backed sandstone bridge that carried a minor road over the Kem Burn, a car stopped and a middle-aged couple got out and leaned on the parapet to watch us float bits of stick on the water. 'That's the most beautiful child I've ever seen,' I heard the woman say in melancholy praise.

Dot ignored them. The woman called 'Cooee!' to attract our attention. When I started to make for the bridge, she shouted to me, 'Is that your sister?' I said no, and she asked me to tell Dot to come over to her.

Dot put down the twig she was using to guide a piece of wood on the water and went to her. A herd of cattle was kept in the field there. On both sides of the Kem there were slopes of trodden, muddy and ungrassed ground where the cows came down to the water's edge to drink. A scab of dried cowpat floated past, and as it neared the bridge, where the current picked up speed, the sun slid from behind a cloud and turned the cowpat golden. The bridge looked so old that I thought I could hear it flake and crumble into the radiant gurgle of the stream.

'She gave me a half crown, and a shilling for you,' Dot said when she came back to me, confused by these gifts. She looked at the coins in the palm of her hand, puzzled by the disparity between them, and then looked back towards the car, whose doors we heard closing. She gave me the half crown. I gave it back to her. 'Don't you want it?' she asked.

'You said she gave it to you.'

'Money from strangers!' Dot spoke with bewilderment. I took the shilling; a child could get a lot for a shilling in those days. 'She said I was the prettiest girl she'd ever seen! I was terrified!' Dot giggled. She looked at the large silver coin. She bit on it. Together, we ran to the roadside where the car was pulling away. The woman was drying her eyes on a handkerchief. It was an all-important mystery – the woman crying, the money, the couple we had never seen before.

For the next hour, we scavenged for more imaginary boats to sail, and discussed how to spend our windfalls.

'If we go to Edwina Gregg's shop, she's bound to ask where we got the money from,' I said. 'Same with the Co-op. But they wouldn't care in the post office.'

'Mrs Graham's in the post office,' Dot said, 'and she knows me. She'll wonder how my mother could've given me a half crown.'

'It's not a lot of money!'

'You should know by now, Alec, that my mother doesn't have *any* money!'

'Well, I get a shilling a week.'

'I know you do, and you've already spent it, so Edwina Gregg would *know*. We'll have to walk to Overrigg, tomorrow,' Dot said.

Dot was invited to stay for tea at our house. In fact, she stayed until past nine o'clock, when my father walked her home. For several weeks, Dot stayed all evening on Mondays and Fridays.

At first, I took it for granted that Dot's visits were the outcome of my father's idea of providing Mrs Gordon with some free evenings for Ralph. But as far as I know, Irene Gordon never went to the pictures or anywhere else with Ralph Harvie. Early in July, he stopped looking after the garden. Dot was mysterious on the subject. When I asked where he was, she said sharply, 'How should I know?'

I never mentioned this to my parents. But one night when he came back from walking Dot home, I heard my father say, 'That Glasgow man has a car. I think it's a Riley.' From his tone I gathered that a Riley was quite a car.

'I feel sorry for Ralph,' said my mother.

'First you call him names for persevering, and now you're sorry for the man? Where did Irene meet this new fellow, anyhow? If you ask me, we shouldn't be looking after Dot while her mother's seeing somebody else!'

My father sounded angry. Genuine concern that Irene Gordon should have a second chance was being forced to fight it out with loyalty to a local man he liked.

'All she told me was she'd met somebody nice, and that she wanted to go out with him,' my mother said. 'I don't know what he does for a living. I don't know his name.' She sounded as upset as my father, but she seemed to be defending Mrs Gordon. 'And don't ask me where he comes from, because I don't know that, either.'

Most women were of the same mind as my mother: they would have been happier to see Irene Gordon accept Ralph, but they admitted with sisterly approval that she had a right to her feelings. Discretion or family ties required some women to take Ralph Harvie's side. A few were scandalized. They accused my mother of harming Ralph by looking after Dot on those evenings.

'I thought it *was* Ralph! Why else would I have offered to keep an eye on Dorothy? And how could I refuse when I found it wasn't?'

Information about Mrs Gordon's boyfriend was gathered piece by piece in Kemshill. Some of it came from me. Dot told me that she had met him, that his name was Clifford Peake, and that he was English. She had kept this news to herself for long enough – that was the impression I got from the way she blurted it out. Several times I had seen women ill-disposed to her mother turn neighbourly charm on Dot, hoping for snippets of fact that her mother had ordered her to keep quiet.

She and I laughed at the strange, high-falutin English name. 'He has a moustache,' Dot cried, 'and you should see the ring he's got! On this finger. It has a red stone.'

My father obviously disapproved of my indiscretion when I started to repeat what Dot confided in me – I could tell by the way he opened his mouth to speak, though he postponed it when my mother looked at him with a shake of the head that told him to shut up.

'You're as curious as I am,' she told him. After that, I refused to divulge what I knew, but they prised it out of me. I told them about the moustache, the ring with the red stone, the man's name.

My mother had already reached the decision that to look after Dorothy would be to implicate herself in the mistake she felt Irene Gordon was making. She had gone to Dot's mother and told her she could no longer help.

Several evenings of the week by then, Clifford Peake's car could be seen parked at a tilt on the bank across the lane from the Gordons' house. On those occasions when Mrs Gordon went out with him, it was to Glasgow, where they dropped Dot off with her aunt and uncle. Dot used to boast about Peake's car, its speed, its upholstery. She talked excitedly about the city. Some days she didn't turn up at school, because she was still in Glasgow. Mrs Gordon no longer shopped in the village. People said she didn't dare show her face in Edwina Gregg's shop or the Co-operative. They prophesied that very soon the Gordons would be moving. They reminisced about Mrs Gordon's parents, and mentioned her mother-in-law, still alive in Overrigg; the word 'if' could be heard on doorsteps, in conversations at corners and outside the shops, in my parents' living room.

Those evenings when Dot had stayed to tea with us, she used to play my mother's piano. My mother could read music a bit, but she couldn't play by ear. Dot could pick up a tune from hearing it, but slowly, and my mother used to sit at the piano with her, teaching her popular songs. It was at these times, I think, that I first detected a change in Dot's behaviour. Always vivacious, she now began to look controlled and pert; her sense of fun seemed less irrepressible and spontaneous, and she appeared conscious of the effect she wanted to make. She had never been shy, but now she seemed willing to affect a charming timidity.

She seemed to have a superior adventure in her life. All of a sudden, she was being whisked off to Glasgow in a fancy car, treated with presents of sweets, new clothes, books, and a bicycle that was too conspicuous for her mother to let her ride it through Kemshill. From having nothing and a sorrowful mother, Dot found herself with plenty, while Irene Gordon dressed smartly and was cheerful, if apprehensive of what Kemshill was saying about her. Dot still turned up to play in my garden, and it didn't take much persuasion for me to go and play in hers. My mother warned me, 'I don't want you there if that man turns up. As soon as you see his car, clear off. Is that understood?'

It's not certain who first passed on the news that Clifford Peake was a married man. Dot never told me that, and I doubt whether she would have told anyone else, even if she knew. My father said the talk would have originated in Overrigg. 'Bad news always starts in Overrigg. I used to think that Hitler might've been an Overrigg man, but I grant you that even Overrigg men aren't *that* bad. Nearly, though.'

'This is serious!' my mother protested.

'It's worse'n that,' my father said, with a smile that disguised his feelings.

From the way my mother bit her lip and her eyes moistened, I gathered that it was the end of the world for Irene Gordon.

But the news seemed to make no difference to Mrs Gordon. If anything, it elicited a courage, or barefacedness, that drove her to visit Kemshill's two shops after an absence of several weeks, and to allow Dot to ride her bicycle wherever she pleased. Clifford Peake's Riley was parked there almost every night now. Dot had a day off school again – she was in Glasgow, with her aunt and uncle – but the car was noticed outside the Gordons' house that next morning. A few days later, Dot asked my mother if she could stay for tea.

'Did your mummy ask you to ask, Dorothy?'

'Yes, she was wondering, Mrs Haddow.'

My mother bit her lower lip and said, 'Wait here with Alec, dear. I'll go and speak to your mother.'

My mother was embarrassed, but Dot's smile was hard and worldly. When my mother reappeared with her coat on, Dot said, 'If you don't want me to stay, Mrs Haddow, just say so, and save yourself a walk.' It sounded impertinent – the remark of a girl older than her eleven years. Worse, to my mother, was that it declared how much Dot knew about what was going on.

Clifford Peake never drove through Kemshill when he went to the Gordons' house or left it at night. He took the narrow back lane that ran past the house and met up with the main road less than a half mile farther on. It was a poorly maintained road, worn thin by agricultural traffic; on summer afternoons around five, it was impassable, jammed with driven cattle, sauntering herd boys and their ill-natured dogs. Most of the time, though, it was deserted. Where the lane joined the main road, the junction was concealed by hedges raised on banks of earth.

Ralph Harvie waited there late one mild, wet October night. When Peake's car stopped at the dark junction, readying itself to nose into the main road, Ralph stepped forward, opened the driver's door, and pulled Peake out.

Gentle, amiable Ralph Harvie – everyone made a point of saying that they had never known him to raise his voice, let alone his hand. I read the newspaper reports and listened to my parents talk. The papers said Peake's head was crushed, not by one unlucky blow but by several. And Ralph himself had called for the ambulance, before waking the local policeman. But, like everyone else in Kemshill, my father refused to believe that Ralph Harvie had left his mother's house that night with thoughts of murder on his mind. In my father's analysis, all Ralph meant to do was warn the fellow off.

'The wrench they're talking about – it must have been in Peake's car. Peake could have come at him with it! Who'd believe that Ralph – of all people – would lie in wait for a man, wi' a wrench, intent on braining him?'

Whatever Ralph meant, events had run out of control. He was strong; he worked in the loading bay at the Rathett Paper Mill. My father expressed the gravity of the matter with his fierce and native 'Ach, ach, ach!'

We were involved: my parents had looked after Dot while her mother went out with Clifford Peake. Two detectives and a uniformed policeman turned up on our doorstep. They were cross-checking dates that Mrs Gordon had given them. I was told to sit in the kitchen, but our house was small, and I could hear without having to put my ear against the door.

'I've known Ralph Harvie for years, and he's not a killer. I'll tell you that for nothing!' My father was always telling people things 'for nothing'. I had never heard him speak with such anger as when he protested against going to Glasgow to testify for the prosecution.

'It's the law, Mr Haddow.' The detective's voice was bored with my father's assertions. 'The Procurator Fiscal might want your evidence in court. You're the man who can verify what Mrs Gordon's said.'

'Me? On the other side from Ralph Harvie?' My father's laugh, rough and incredulous, taunted the policeman.

'A man's dead, Mr Haddow!'

* * *

Irene Gordon took Dot and went to her sister's in Glasgow for the duration of the trial. It was well she stayed clear of Kemshill – those who objected to Mrs Gordon's choice of a lover were vociferous in heaping the blame on her head. Anyone who had granted her freedom to choose now changed his mind. But, being devoted to Dot, I was tormented by not seeing her, or knowing what she felt. Something had changed between us, something that no adult platitude or juvenile insight could utter clearly.

Ralph was sentenced to hang. The town was outraged. On appeal, the sentence was reduced to life imprisonment, and Kemshill was still angry. Laws were held in contempt. A neighbour of ours struck his wife, who left him. The local constable was ostracized, and had to be replaced. His stout adolescent son, known as Biscuit Belly, was beaten up behind the bus shelter, and he named the boys who did it.

The townsfolk went over the case in detail until the subject was exhausted. 'Ralph's mother can't take it in.' 'That poor Mrs Peake – what a story to hear told in a court!' 'This village was never in the papers – now look at us! Irene Gordon's seen to that!'

'They're laughing at Kemshill in Overrigg,' my father said. 'But then, that's what they're like in Overrigg. They've always been jealous.'

Dot and Mrs Gordon came back after the trial. Dot told me they would have stayed on longer with her aunt, but the two women argued all the time, and her uncle threw the Gordons out.

Tall, cream-coloured curds rose on the bolted seedstalks of the Gordons' rhubarb that next summer. Left unharvested the previous year, vegetables that Ralph had planted reseeded themselves, and now they ran wild; Irene Gordon had dug up no more than a handful of potatoes, and let the weeds smother the rest of the garden.

It was good to have Dot back again; I had been convinced she was gone for good. And despite the feeling in Kemshill, my mother encouraged me not to turn my back on Dot. For her own part, she sometimes gave me a basket of produce to pass on to Mrs Gordon, but these discreet kindnesses were as far as she would go. For the moment, she could not bring herself to resurrect their old friendship, although I imagine there were times when she thought she should.

I remember Dot's mother, that autumn, hanging her washing in the rain, tramping down the overgrown wet grass to get at her weathered clothes rope. It could hang there for days on end. Whenever she saw me, she scowled.

No one spoke to Mrs Gordon in the street. Shabby, unkempt, she looked the way she had before Peake arrived in her life – or she in his, however it was. To do her irregular errands, she ran the gauntlet of the houses and entered the furnace of Edwina Gregg's little shop. Some animosity fell on Dot from the young people, too, but she turned up her nose at the hostility and walked away. She seemed undamaged by the drama that afflicted her house. Her young dignity seemed very grown up to me. Neither she nor her mother seemed to mourn Clifford Peake. Ironically, the village that had deplored her interest in Peake was now incensed at her present indifference.

'I think she should move,' my mother said. 'It would be better for her and everyone else.'

'Overrigg would have her,' my father said, and my mother frowned at his flippancy.

'Lawrie Gordon's brother lives in Overrigg,' she pointed out, 'and his mother, too – old Mrs Gordon. That's hardly a fresh start!'

'Now, if they'd done what family should've done in Irene's circumstances, all this might never've happened.'

'Were you a friend of Dot's dad?' I asked him once.

'I knew Lawrie, but I wasn't a pal. Anybody wi' any sense waited to be called up, but no' Lawrie Gordon – he volunteered the minute the war started. Dorothy would've been a year old. He was on leave for two or three weeks, and then he was off to the Far East. And that was that.'

Secondary school separated me from Dot. We went to the same school, in a town ten miles away, but she made new friends; none of them were from anywhere around Kemshill. On the bus home one day, she told me, 'We might be moving, Alec. My mum's been to see a flat in Glasgow.'

'Soon? I don't think I'd like living in Glasgow.'

'Oh, no, it's wonderful! I used to love staying with my aunt and uncle! Now they're just as bad as the people here. They need somebody to blame, other than the man who actually did it.' There was no bitterness in her voice, only experience.

But indecision, indolence and depression kept Irene Gordon in Kemshill. Often when I called to see Dot, she was not there but visiting her new friends in the town where we went to school. When I did find her at home, we used to sit in the kitchen, and her mother would pass silently in and out, chain-smoking and brewing endless cups of tea – she put twice as many leaves in the pot as my mother did. Only occasionally – say, if the mobile shop from Overrigg sounded its horn on the lane outside – would she perk up, animated by an event that snapped her out of her contemplative lethargy. The house was a mess: unwashed dishes and piles of laundry cluttered the kitchen, and the table was never cleared. On it there was a bread-board, and what was left of a loaf. Stale crumbs spilled over the plastic tablecloth, with its holes at each corner where triangles of wooden table peeped through.

'Look at the state she lets this place get into!' Dot said to me. 'She's always complaining about it. I do my best, but look at it! Half the time she hardly knows I'm here. She forgets things. Well, when you think of it, what's she got to remember?'

Again, there was no resentment in Dot's voice as she described her mother's incompetence. Any mild indignation she might feel she made part of this comic state of affairs; it was as if Dot laughed at her own circumstances, disapproving of the near-squalor of her house and yet accepting it – one more feature of her life that made her different from the rest of us.

Over the next three years, I suppose I called on Dot a half-dozen times a year, finding her at home less often than not. It was a friendship I was unable to let go.

Dot was a figure at school; she was bright, and she was theatrical and lively. She was known for mimicry and music, playing the piano at lunch hour in the Senior Girls' Common Room, hammering out the hit tunes of the day.

When I succeeded in visiting her, I saw that Dot's mother took no interest in her progress at school. Instead, she seemed to take it for granted that her sixteen-year-old daughter would be cleverer than most. I noticed an arrogance in the way Irene Gordon lived with her misfortunes and poverty. There was a calculating sneer, too, in the way she looked at me. Her contempt was puzzling. Perhaps she saw me as a representative of my mother, her former friend. When she asked about my mother, she looked at me coldly. Maybe she meant me to feel that she considered my mother disloyal. But there was more to Irene Gordon's bitterness than that. Everyone else in Kemshill walked past the Gordons' house as if it did not exist, or as if they considered it a place blighted and effaced from the map.

When I saw Dot now, it was usually on the bus home from school. As we got off one day deep in a conversation she had started, I asked, 'Does she ever mention your father?'

'You certainly pick your moments, Alec!'

We were crossing the road opposite where Ralph Harvie had killed Clifford Peake. I apologized, and Dot laughed at my sincerity and poor timing.

'I'll tell you how to start a new scandal,' Dot whispered mischievously. If you're seen carrying my satchel up the road . . .' She nodded towards the hedge; behind it, an unidentifiable figure was scything grass. 'No, she never mentions my father, or hardly ever. I wish I could remember him, though. I can't say I ever knew him.'

Irene Gordon was forty – Dot and I were in our final year at school – when she started to work, in the canteen at the Rathett Paper Mill. My father raised his eyebrows and showed the palms of his hands to heaven – or the ceiling – as he groaned at the woman's irresponsible folly: that was where Ralph Harvie had worked, and he had friends there.

Dot hated her mother's newfound jauntiness. 'I don't want to talk about it!' she said, when all I did was mention that the kitchen had been redecorated. 'The last thing I want's my mother making more bad feeling in this place when I'm getting ready to sit exams!'

'I don't see how you can be angry . . .'

'Look, no one can say that my mother's done much for me. We've hardly had two pennies to rub together since I was born. There was plenty of money, once – you know who I'm talking about. But she never took the trouble to earn anything before. I'll tell you why she's taken that particular job: she's trying to make life worse than it already is. It's taken her four or five years to figure out how to go about it. What's she *doing*?'

'Everybody says your mother's looking much better.'

'Huh! *Everybody says!*'

'Honest, I think they're genuine. You should be glad that maybe they're willing to change their minds –'

'They don't know what to think,' Dot said.

In the canteen, Mrs Gordon encountered a customer who discovered who she was. He asked sly questions about how Ralph was getting along. Some reports claimed that she was slow to retaliate; others said that she endured the man's provocation for less than a minute before she lost her temper. There was a violent scene, and the management invited Mrs Gordon to lift her insurance card and other papers and leave their employ.

When I passed the news to my father, he looked up from his gladioli bed – two dozen emergent shoots, neatly labelled – and listened. 'I'm sorry to hear it, but I can't say I'm surprised. That's why she went there.' He brushed aside my questions as to what he meant and how he knew.

I went to see Dot, worried about this new development. 'There are other jobs! There are plenty of jobs!' her mother told me gaily. 'You can tell your saintly mother that I'm not sorry about what happened. And tell her I won't need her baskets of vegetables this year. I can look after myself. Tell her I've changed in a way she wouldn't even understand!'

There were parcels on the kitchen table. Irene Gordon began to untie one of them. Dot turned abruptly away. I sensed that the two had been quarrelling before I arrived. 'Wouldn't you say I've been hard done by, Alec?' Mrs Gordon demanded.

'I think you should keep Alec out of this,' Dot said from the sink.

'I'm talking to you, Alec! Hard done by – wouldn't you say so?'

I agreed with her.

Dot rushed up behind me and began pushing me towards the door.

'Don't you send him away, Dorothy! Alec, you arrived in the nick of time! I was about ready to wring her neck!' she cried.

Dot went back to the sink. Her mother dragged a dress from its parcel. Tissue paper floated in the room and settled on the floor as Mrs Gordon held the dress against her. 'What do you think, Dorothy?'

'I think it stinks!'

Dorothy pushed past me, opened the door, and went out. Her mother scowled at me with vindictive triumph.

After the examinations, there was little reason to go back to school except for the company; I took afternoons off. Once, on the noon bus, I found Dot Gordon reading, and we spent that afternoon together in the Gordons' neglected garden. Then we spent several more afternoons there – leisurely, loafing, tea-drinking afternoons. Time passed very slowly.

'It's sometimes the back of eleven before she gets home, sometimes much later. I waited up on Tuesday night,' Dot said. 'She was drunk. I'm sure she's got another boyfriend. How'd you like it if your mother were seen plastered on the last bus? We had a terrible row, Alec. She tells me, 'I've scrimped and saved and done without, for what? For you to go to university? Don't make me laugh."

I had nothing to confess about either of my parents that might help Dot feel less exceptional. I felt safe, coddled in averageness, affection and security, none of which Dot had ever enjoyed. At best, I could have said that my father was a political half-wit who had recently devised a theory that the compulsory study of flower and vegetable cultivation in all schools world-wide would save the planet from the madness of its rulers. My complaint seemed too trivial to counter Dot's accounts about her mother. And besides, I'd begun to suspect that Dot enjoyed being exceptional.

'She isn't finished yet,' Dot said. 'In fact, she's hardly started. And I'll tell you this – I don't care what she does, because I won't be here to have to live with it.'

Dot planned to share a flat with other students at the university. She was determined to leave home. 'She's got another job, as a waitress, and she can't claim that she needs me. And I don't need her,' she said calmly. 'I mean, she won't help me, and no one else will. I'll just make my own way.' It was the unruffled determination of her attitude that agitated me most.

'Leave home now and you could make your mother do something daft,' I said anxiously. 'You'd blame yourself.'

Her patience with me, her suppressed laugh that recalled her mother's face as it prepared for a downright scowl, seemed to accuse me of lacking perspicacity. 'I don't even like her,' Dot said. 'She's never made me feel that she wants me here. She told me herself she can't stand the sight of me.' These were unforgiving words, and they disturbed me. 'I wouldn't tell you this, Alec, unless she already knew what I think about her. I've told her what I have in mind. You don't know the half of it.' I was ready to believe her. 'We haven't said a civil word to each other in months. Neither of us can be bothered to even try.'

It took several days before I brought myself to confide in my father.

'You'll be worried about Dorothy, but I wouldn't worry too much, son. After an upbringing like that, she'll stand on her own two feet all right. I'm as sure of that as I've been sure of anything else in this world. Anyway, Dot's hardly the first young woman to make a break for it.'

'Did you already know it had come to this?'

'No, I didn't, but I could see it coming.'

'How could you tell?'

He paused as he firmed a plant in a pot. 'When water runs off that glass,' he said, looking up at the roof of his greenhouse, 'then I know it's raining.'

'I know Dot better than almost anyone, and it didn't strike *me* as obvious.'

'No, nobody sees what's happening to somebody they're fond of,' he said, with irritating judiciousness. 'A twisted minx she'll grow up to be, unless we've a miracle, and miracles don't happen. It's you I'm worried about. I know where you've been every afternoon this week.'

'Don't go round thinking it's like that.'

'Maybe not, but you'd like it to be.' I turned my face away. 'Do something about it,' he said. 'And if you take my advice, it'll be a goodbye.'

When I next saw Dot, I noticed a playful tolerance in her manner. Occasionally she showed signs of boredom as I talked about books or movies. Her intelligence was quick and brilliant; it was unlike her to say so little. She seemed to be waiting for me to take a step that she had predicted weeks or months before. Now, and probably then, too, I had a sense of inevitable ending – that I would touch her, kiss her, and that doing so would break all of childhood like a sheet of glass. I felt that Dot was enduring my reticence, putting up with me, her eyes daring me forward with their keen blue challenge that said she would not make the first move, that it was all up to me. When I kissed her, Dot's complicity was unmistakable; her willingness felt as real as my own. But after a minute or two she pushed me away and got up from the grass. Her composure was remarkable; mine was less so, but at least it was composure: my father had not forewarned me in so many words, but he had hinted at how it would turn out.

Dot said, 'I've too much on my mind to get involved, and you and I probably *would* get all mixed up about this.'

She seemed surprised that I walked away without clumsy, amorous talk. She called after me as I swung the gate behind me. It squeaked worse than ever.

Before Dot left Kemshill early in September, there were reports of arguments late at night between her and her mother. After she'd gone, the stories continued, supplied by evening dog-walkers and furtive drunks, the bearers of whispers. Irene Gordon was seen on the last bus, they said: sometimes accompanied by a man, often abusive, well dressed, made up, smart and tight. Over the next years her looks, rescued from the past, succumbed to time and age. As she withered into pathos, repentance and loneliness, my mother and a few of her friends took to visiting her again.

Ralph Harvie was released after serving ten years of his sentence. When he came out of prison he had the good sense not to settle in Kemshill. Before moving farther away, he stayed for a few months in Overrigg. My father's humour survived a little longer. 'Overrigg? But Ralph, you were innocent.'

'George, I was guilty. I killed a man.'

'But Overrigg? That's too much punishment.'

Ralph waved away my father's jovial efforts. 'I meant to kill him. I thought of very little else ever since the day I knew he existed.'

It was six years before I saw Dot again; she called my name across a street in Glasgow. It was as though she had just been on my mind; perhaps she always was. The pale fineness of her skin had gone. There were faint lines running from her inner cheeks into the corners of her mouth. She looked older and different, but still persisting within her was the outline of the indestructible friend of my childhood. Perhaps I was the only person alive who could see that. She kissed me on the cheek, and said I could buy her coffee. I bought her dinner. Then the rest of it started.

THE SEVEN FARMS

From the eastern heights of the valley – which aren't very high – you can see almost the entire course of the river. With the aid of patience and binoculars you could reach an almost exact count of anglers, bridges, herons and swans, except for a stretch of about half a mile where the bank is steep and wooded. Look left, to the south, and most of a town can be seen. Walk slightly further and higher on the quiet road, and then look right, and there's a good view of the small estuary. To earn a better view of the sea and the larger town beside it means walking and climbing for a mere ten minutes more. A lot of just about everything can be observed in a short space of time involving very little effort. It's a small country. This district is one of its many miniatures.

Several small villages can be seen. There are a few unpleasant exceptions but for the most part the red-roofed tiles of new bungalows look as if they've lost a battle with modernity and pulled back with a blush into the same eras as the older dwellings. Old men and women walk on that minor road in the summer evenings. Watching them in that state of mind which distrusts the complacency of the district can lead to the suspicion that a comfortable arrangement between yesterday and now might be what these elderly strollers hope to have negotiated. They look at the peaceful valley as if they've forgotten most of what's happened to them and almost everything they've read in the newspapers or seen on television. Experience and news rarely coincide there. A satisfaction of the place is that it's both attractive and unremarkable. Almost anything disagreeable, unsavoury or vexing can be understated by slow degrees until it vanishes.

Dr David Findlater was unsure of his reasons for choosing to go back there during his summer break. An unsentimental man, he was aware of having taken a decision that was out of character. He felt that he was behaving badly towards himself. Rootlessness was an explanation that crossed his mind; but he thought it a matter for contempt that he should have allowed even an instinctive fear of deracination to have disturbed his usual calm. Personal crises, of which he'd known a few, were always explicable, no matter the pain and sorrow they caused. It felt disreputable and silly that he should find himself returning self-indulgently to where he'd been born and brought up, a place he'd left almost thirty-seven years before at the age of sixteen. He took comfort from the knowledge that only he could tell what he was up to, except that he didn't know exactly. There was an introspective mischief about his half-intended, reluctant reunion with his past.

Part of the unsettling enjoyment he took from his costly suite of bedroom, sitting room and bathroom arose – there was no doubt about it – from the fact that the hotel had once been the house that dominated his father's life, his mother's, his brother's, his sister's, and his own. It was less than 800 yards from the house in which he'd been born and raised; and the house of the proprietor of the seven farms was now a hotel! Dr Findlater wished he could resurrect his parents to tell them that. Not, though, that they could be imagined for a single moment agreeing to be put up for a few nights in Strathuden House, hotel or no hotel.

In the summer of 1955, when the Findlaters left, they went with the momentum of rancour. 'Nothing else for it,' Dr Findlater's father had said. 'Strike out for new pastures.' It was like his father not to have said 'pastures new'. Had a farm-worker's irony been encrusted on that ornamental word 'pastures'? It wasn't appreciated that Findlater's father spoke out on the subject of wages and enlisted the union to help him. Gilnickie – yes, these toytown Scottish names! – wasn't farmed by a tenant like the others, but by a manager put there by the estate's owner. Some of the farm-workers on the seven farms agreed with Findlater, but only in private. Others thought him a trouble-maker. Life was made awkward. There were accusations of pilfering – hens, eggs, seed potatoes, tools and the like. 'Nothing else for it,' his father said, his laughing cadences lilting with resignation more than belligerence, his discontent disguised by a forced good nature. Dr Findlater remembered coming home from school on his bicycle to see the man who once lived in Strathuden House shout at his father, 'Look for a job in your own time, not in mine!' Findlater thought of his father as curiously undefeated and yet incapable of wrath; and, ever since, he'd tried to work out the puzzle of his father's temperament, one in which principle and conviction refused the temptations of acrimony or even vehemence put in its way by a vindictive opponent. But perhaps Dr Findlater was perplexed by his own equable outlook on life, having seen disease and death during most of his working days.

There was a clear view of the farm cottages from his sitting-room window. He'd looked at them late that afternoon with his binoculars, which, that evening, he'd then trained on the anglers, bridges, herons, swans and other birds on the river when he'd walked up the high road after an early dinner. Now that he was back in his suite he focused on a low terrace which had been knocked into one elongated house, re-roofed, rebuilt, with a substantial garden, and a garage added at one side. His plan had been to visit it earlier in the evening. Instead, he'd taken a path to the minor road that ran under the upper ridge of the valley. He was booked in for a week. He didn't want to rush. But at the same time he knew his planned walk was postponed by a memory. On the day he left with his family there had been an argument about a potted geranium which his mother had left inside on a window sill. 'For luck?' his father asked. 'It'll die of thirst. What's the luck in that?' 'No luck, or bad luck,' his mother answered with a malice that surprised him. 'None for him who's pushin' us off. None for them as come in after us.' He remembered the geranium looking like an emblem of a curse. 'Don't blame *him*,' his father said to his mother, his reproach sounding too reasonable. Findlater's brother and sister were too young to understand much of what was happening. 'He's been moochin' around for a place for months.' He meant the man who'd be leading his family into the cottage in a couple of weeks' time. Their opportunity arose from the Findlaters' misfortune. 'So?' his mother said in the spoken shorthand that existed between her and Dr Findlater's father. 'I'll find a place for it on the back of the lorry,' his father said patiently. Time and delays never seemed to matter much to him. 'I doubt if they'd want it,' he said to a look of his mother's that suggested they give the plant to one of their two neighbours. He'd wondered often what his father meant. Presumably the significance of a presented geranium would have come across like an insult – 'Remember us by this, when we're intent on forgetting *you*.' It ended up under the tarpaulin of the lorry from Annan, where they were headed – 'Far enough away!' his father had said contentedly.

His sister was squeezed into the cabin on her mother's knee, beside his brother and the driver, an obliging man who all that morning agreed to everything asked of him with a succession of 'Aye', or 'Fine', or 'We'll get it in somehow.' He and his father stood on the running-boards of the old, over-laden truck, holding on to the inside of the doors, one on either side. Men, boys and women were haymaking in a field – not one of Gilnickie's, but belonging to one of the seven farms, which meant the same landowner. No one waved. Once off the unmacadamed farm road they drove to the station in the town. For a family that had travelled nowhere on holiday, it felt like a serious departure as Findlater and his father waved to the truck when it left the railway station. There was a momentary sensation of the family being split up, and Findlater hadn't forgotten that imagined, more extreme circumstance, followed by several hours when he had his father's company to himself.

Inspection through binoculars from his hotel window hadn't prepared him for the elongated affluence of the house he thought he knew and which he now stood beside. It was as different from itself as Strathuden House from the hotel it had become. Each dwelling once had four small rooms. Now it had been made one house and even at close range he couldn't tell exactly how the interior looked. A large extension had been added at the rear as well as the garage for two cars at one side. From the growth of shrubs and trees Dr Findlater guessed that the cottages had been rebuilt ten or fifteen years previously, long enough ago, at any rate, for their opulent unfamiliarity to confuse the memory he had of them. 'Put this place away,' part of his mind said. 'Why did you come back when it was already behind you?' Elation competed with disappointment. He asked himself if he'd really expected to see the same cottages and evidence of the same living conditions he'd known when he was young. Through a half-open window a radio transmitted a voice and then the music of the here-and-now. He smiled at the involuntary mutation of the music into the sounds of his mother's wireless in the early 1950s after electricity was led into the cottages. Double glazing, neatly pointed brickwork, wisteria and clematis beginning to fade and wither, honeysuckle coming into full flower, roses, and the scent of grass very recently mown – it was years, but a distance of more than time, from his home, and yet it was where his home had been and, in a perplexing geographical sense if none other, where it still was. Between his memory and what he stood there and witnessed were years of occasional, sharp reminiscences, many of them happy, but all of them shadowed by the conclusive soreness of their last weeks there. Perplexed by the discreet turbulence he felt, Dr Findlater was conscious of an additional source of confusion which was as unlike him as confusion itself – envy. In the course of its social history, its promotion from the dwellings of farm-labourers to the single house of whatever comfortably off family now lived in it, the house of his birth looked like the house in the country of which he'd dreamt increasingly over the past couple of years. His hospital consultancy in London provided a growing nest-egg which a man who worked hard, lived simply and on his own had rarely had the chance to ponder, and never the time to spend. Property, like money, didn't enter his priorities. Now, though, he stood outside a significant house and coveted it: he felt mortified by a lapse of taste.

'Can I help you?' It was a woman's voice. She repeated her question. She was forceful and emphatic. Dr Findlater was jolted from his thoughts and it took him a few seconds to find where she stood in the garden, only a few yards in front of him but partly hidden by the long, loose branches of a buddleia. 'What do you want?' She was in her mid-thirties and dressed for outdoors in shorts and a loose T-shirt. A boy of about four stood beside her holding on shyly to her tanned leg.

'I didn't mean to startle you,' Dr Findlater said over the waist-high white fence. Instinctively, he took a few steps towards the gate. His straw hat, which he now held in his hand, his blue linen jacket, white shirt, silk tie, off-white trousers and polished brogues would have suggested to just about anyone that he was a man of a certain assured style which settled on him naturally or as a consequence of income or professional status, even if imitated unthinkingly – as in Findlater's case – from admired senior colleagues now dead or retired. But the woman's indignant self-confidence ignored the signals sent out by his demeanour and clothes.

'You've been looking at this house for ages and I can't think *why*,' she said. 'I take it you can read? Then it says in very plain words on the notice' – she pointed towards the road-end – '*Private Road*.' Her voice identified her as English. Dr Findlater supposed that after so many years in London a quality of sound more than an accent determined the nationality of how he spoke. What survived in his mouth was nothing like the voice of the place where he was born and brought up. He sometimes talked it to himself or to Scots nurses in the hospital, as if in mutual code or an agreed, shared, spoken cuddle. 'Private Road – it's a very clear phrase. Isn't it?'

'I'm extremely sorry to have . . .'

'Half the houses round here have been broken into . . .' she said angrily.

'Well, it's always been a private road,' he said. 'Or it always used to be.'

'We've been broken into!'

'But it didn't mean 'keep out.' It was more an excuse for the potholes, or a case of 'on your own head be it.''

'Are you a local?'

'No. Not exactly. But . . .'

'Then I'll ring the police if you don't go at once.'

What someone else in the same position as Dr Findlater might have said would be along the lines of, 'I am an oncologist of international repute, a Fellow of the Royal College of Surgeons, a Fellow of This, That and the Next Thing, and I was born here.' Anything as politely rebarbative or assertive was beyond him. Instead, he began to back off, finding himself concerned for whatever causes underlay the woman's animated ire, her evident distress. He was used to disquiet in men and women; he'd had to tell them things about themselves which put their self-control under serious strain, with all sorts of predictable and unpredictable reactions. 'I'm very sorry. I'm very sorry, indeed.'

'Get away from here!' There was a unnerving control behind the ferocity of her snapped command.

Dr Findlater made a placating gesture with his hands, smiled at the little boy, and walked away. A moment later he heard a door slam.

Clearly, he thought, I look nothing like a thief. She's realized her mistake, but she's too proud to apologize. It's her manner. Besides, having been broken into, and robbed of God knows what, maybe with all sorts of unpleasant mess, she must be in a bit of a state. Understandable. Understandable, but bloody disappointing.

It was preposterous! Was that house, that road, the entire district, accursed? As soon as someone called Findlater appeared on the scene there was a struggle with someone laying down the law and exercising proprietorial rights. Could anyone escape from the significance of their original circumstances? To have gone back there was humiliating enough without being addressed as a possible thief – he couldn't remember a single crime of that kind in his childhood – threatened with the police, and told to clear off. He stopped on a stretch of the road that was shaded on one side by elder trees – 'boortrees', his father called them. The shade was welcome. What should he do? Listen to his silent, rueful chuckles, his deserved rebuff, and learn from them? Or give in to the resentment which he also felt? Odd, he thought, that the membrane separating private amusement from secret anger should be so fragile. Odder still that some of us seem so disgustingly sane that we can control – or think we can – the passion that turns one into the other or mixes them up.

He was diverted by details of the roadside. Elder-flowers, dog-roses, grasses, led him to stop. He looked closely at what were once familiar minutiae – stones of a wall taken down long before his childhood, signs of lapsed fencing (some rotten posts, a few rusted strands of barbed wire), spaces in the thick hawthorns through which he'd pressed himself many times as a boy. His memory was clear and seemed part of present reality. Of course it was.

He remembered a reasonably distinguished colleague saying, when drunk, as they tried to find a taxi, 'I wouldn't go so far as to claim that I am pre-eminent in the profession. But one of its ornaments? Does that sound fair?' To which, Findlater – wincing and sober – had forced an answer: 'Yes, Peter. Strikes me as more than fair.' At the time he'd felt that his colleague's vanity, insecurity, or whatever it was, deserved a kick up the backside. But why had that footling episode come back to him? He supposed it might be a substitute, or explanation, for the riposte he hadn't been able to make to the woman a quarter of an hour before. How could I say to a woman who's obviously preyed on by highly understandable anxieties, 'I beg your pardon, but in point of fact I'm as glowing an example of Local Boy Makes Good as you'll find in these parts?' She must feel bad enough without my rubbing it in. But his frustration was large; it overtook him and met him farther along the road, where he felt it necessary to sit down on a low mound of stones and try to cool off. Agricultural machinery was baling a field nearby but the sight of it was hidden by a walled bank topped with a hawthorn hedge through which crab-apple trees grew. His hands were fisted; his fingernails dug into the soft lower parts of his palms. He took deep breaths, rolled his shoulders, and shook his hands loose in search of relaxation. He could see the hotel in the distance – Strathuden House Hotel that had been Strathuden House. Greenhouses reflected the sun in silent salvos. Stands of timber looked majestic and permanent as if almost forty years hadn't made a blind bit of difference to the power and ownership of which they were tokens.

He began walking back the way he'd come. Am I hoping for a chance to clear up this embarrassment and put that woman's mind at rest as well as my own? Or am I too tired to go the long way round?

A sense of how livings are made from land lingered in him, even if it was a reduced, half-forgotten instinct, several pulses out of seventy-two. He was surprised at himself. He loved and hated the sight of expert agriculture around him. The baler drove by above him with its invisible noisiness.

'You've been looking at this house for ages and I can't think *why*.' How long did I actually stand there? Why did she say 'for ages'? Wasps crowded around their nest hung high in the hedge. A subdued, intent, obsessive hum whispered over the road; it was a miracle of intuitive diligence. Dedication and getting on with the job until the day you die. No beating about the bush for these little chaps. No fancy dithering, either, about whether you're a paragon or whether it's 'fair' to opt for the rank of 'ornament'. Why must some people insist on treating others as if they were servants? Or as if from the vantage of superiority? *Did* I hang about outside her house for as long as she said? What's it called? A 'raptus'? Busy medical scientists, with patients, research work on hand, students and umpteen honorary professorships, aren't prone to day-dreaming and losing a sense of time. He punctured his misgivings, then re-inflated them. Perhaps I did. I have to admit it – I was stunned by the changes to the place. I knew in advance it wouldn't look anything like my memories. Outside lavatory, getting washed at the kitchen sink, water heated on the coal-fired range, electricity only in our last five years (my father trimming wicks on the lamps, yellow light pulsing on the pages of a book). Why do I remember these things?

He wasn't yet visible from the house. 'You've been looking at this house for ages and I can't think *why*.' He could feel her voice, its pronunciation, as if it were just out of earshot. He was hot; his throat was dry and he sweated. He fanned himself with his hat then loosened his shirt under the armpits and plucked it from his chest in an attempt to air himself. Please, don't tell me I'm about to explain myself to her! I should never have come here. There was the straight road leading to the highway. The argument over the pot-plant. Standing on the running-board of a ramshackle lorry from Annan loaded with plain, simple belongings. Being dropped at the station with my father. His purse. He always carried money in a purse! The fares already measured and the exact sum handed over. An eternal gesture of a family reduced to its last few pounds. Fingers in a purse. An exact knowledge of how much was in it – counted, measured. So much for this, so much for that, and very little left over for anything else. The train to Edinburgh. My father in a green tweed suit loosening his tie in the compartment and saying, 'Might as well be comfortable. An hour to wait at Edinburgh Waverley,' and that information having been told to him several times before in the past few days. His father winking at him – 'It'll be much the same, only different.' No, can't forget it. But that's no reason to come back. A man, in my circumstances, from my background, my very precise background in terms of this place and that absolutely specific house, comes home . . . And instead of . . . instead of whatever, he feels a disgrace to himself! He feels ashamed! He feels disgusted because he let it happen. She's probably right. I was rooted to the spot. I stood outside her relatively remote house, where she's alone with a child, for what would have seemed to her an inordinately long time . . . Or did I?

Once again he was astonished by the conversion of a three-cottage terrace into a single house. Only someone who'd known it intimately, who'd lived in it, whose eyes had grown up looking at everything around it, could measure the fullness of its metamorphosis from the homes of the low-paid to the residence of those who'd done well out of recent time. 'I wouldn't go so far as to claim that I am pre-eminent in the profession. But one of its ornaments? Does that sound fair?' 'Yes, Peter. Strikes me as more than fair.' Why are people vain instead of getting on with doing what they do? Why do they barge, elbow, malign and deceive each other? Why is honesty booted from the room in order to leave more space for self-interest? He approached the gate with his hat in one hand, fanning his face, and his handkerchief in the other, dabbing at his brow. Opening it would have been overstepping the mark. Yes, he thought, the only 'nice man' is one who agrees with you or does as you say, one who lets you be boss or allows himself a role as second best. 'Excuse me!' he called. 'Is anyone there?' To be considered 'kind' these days you have to be subordinate or servile. 'Hello! Hello!' Or you mustn't rock *his* boat, but when he rocks yours you say, 'Thank you, Peter.' An ornament? Then an incompetent one, and lazy with it.

He saw the woman at the window nearest him. 'Could I have a word, please?' he said, over-mouthing the words for the sake of the glass between them. 'There's been a misunderstanding!' She opened the window and he repeated what he'd said. He brought out his wallet and held up his card. 'I'm not a thief and I'm not selling anything!' he called out. He was shocked by how declarative and firm he was being. 'I'm a doctor, as it happens. This is my card. Do you want me to bring it to the window?'

She closed the window and disappeared. Oh, no, I hope that stupid woman's not about to phone the police. He was too tensed by the effort of speaking to her from the gate to reach conclusions about what to read from her face at the window. She came round the side of the house followed by her son.

'I'm very sorry . . .'

'What do you mean by this?'

'Maybe my card will reassure you . . .'

'I don't care who or what you are.'

'You'd a perfect right to feel spooked,' he conceded. She was looking at him with what he considered to be excessive concern. 'I'm sorry about that. But I was born in that house. I hadn't seen it in nearly forty years. I was surprised. Actually, more than surprised, but I don't know how to tell you . . .' She took his card and stepped back. 'It's very different. To be truthful, it was a shock to me. You see, when I say it's different, I mean much more than that. I mean totally, totally changed, and I feel as if my memories' – oh, no, what a soppy, wet word it sounds, accompanied by languorous violins – 'have been stolen, or chastised . . .'

'Are you all right?'

'Fine. Yes. I wouldn't say no to a glass of water. The heat,' he said. 'Shock, too, I dare say.'

She ran inside at a speed that struck him as over-solicitous. He fanned himself briskly with his hat. 'What's your name?' he said to the little boy, who walked off and sat on his tricycle on the path.

The woman returned quickly with a glass of water and gave it to him.

He drank half the glass in a single gulp. 'Never a good idea to drink too quickly when over-heated. What they say in the films is quite right. Not that I've been crawling across the Sahara for a week.' He took a sip. 'When was it rebuilt?'

'In 1980, 1979 . . .' she said, thinking aloud. 'Twelve years ago. I think it was more or less derelict for a while.'

'And you've lived here for . . .?'

'Five years. Are you sure you're all right?'

'Fine.' He sipped more water. 'You said I stood here for ages. Did I?'

'Yes. Why would I say it if you hadn't?'

'There were three cottages. We lived at this end – there. Not like your house. Nothing like. All three tenants were farmworkers. Two of the families were more or less transient. Here for a year or two and then off. One day you'd have friends to play with, and then you wouldn't. A couple who lived at that end for several months had five of a family. Five. Not much in the way of toys, either, I remember. They used to play with old shoe-boxes and Ostermilk tins, soap packets, and they'd a couple of biscuit tins, a gas mask and a soldier's helmet. I was very jealous of that soldier's helmet,' he said to the little boy. 'Very jealous, I can tell you! Thank you for the water.'

She opened the gate. 'Won't you come in?' He smiled, thinking that he heard her cross a verbal obstacle.

'I'd better get back before they finish serving the expensive lunch I've already paid for,' he said. He wanted to admit, 'If I'm in this mess by looking at the outside of the old place, can you imagine me browsing through your tasteful interior without cracking up entirely?' But he said, 'No, that's very kind, but I mustn't,' and hoped she'd see the truth on his face. 'Delightful child. You must be very proud.'

'He was born here too.'

'Ah. Another native of the house.'

'My husband's at home all day on Wednesday. I'm sure he'd like to meet you.'

He declined the invitation with a smile and a flutter of his hands. He walked away for a few yards, stopped, turned round, and said, 'Goodbye. Thank you for the water.'

'What does the 'D' stand for?' She held up his card.

'David.'

She nodded.

When he turned to look back a hundred yards along the straight road, almost against his will, she was standing out on the road and her son was on his trike. She waved, and Findlater waved. 'Goodbye,' he said quietly. 'Goodbye.'

MORE THAN HALF THE WAY

Rent was low, life was quiet in the country. It suited Harriet Mortimer to live there. Her small, inexpensive cottage was comfortable and no more. She had perfected her thirty-three years of widowhood in its few rooms. When her son Christopher left home it was like the addition of one last touch to her fastidious grief.

First he had gone to university and then to London. By now he was nearer, in a town fifty miles north. He was as tall as his father had been and he had the same appearance of an athlete who had given up his regimen and on whom late nights, tobacco and alcohol were beginning to catch up. Neither of them had been particularly athletic, and, now, Christopher was a decade older than the age his father was when he had been killed in the last weeks of war by frightened German boys, almost, Harriet had been told, by mistake. She had looked at her son on his sixteenth birthday and thought of these German teenagers and relished the dispiriting, European irony. Her husband, Gareth Mortimer, a war poet, would have approved of how Harriet noticed these coincidences that cumulate into a grotesquely amusing sadness, a grin before terror. It was a mystifying circumstance for Harriet and her son that he was now ten years older than his father had ever been. She could see Gareth in Christopher, her husband shadowed in her son who was now thickening at the waist. Her tall Sunday visitor wore his face set in a projection of gentle bemusement. He looked as if he acknowledged the world through the weariness of an amiably melancholic man older than his years. Those who knew he was the son of Gareth Mortimer were quick to read a wonderingly profound sensitivity into his range of expressions. He never swore; he did not raise his voice or lose his temper. His saddening eyes were easily distracted by the sight of something vague in the distance.

Reports of those cut down in chance explosions –
For ever more now, they are nocturnal roses
In abstract gardens whitening with loss.

These lines from one of Gareth's poems often came into Harriet's head. It was an unpublished poem and she kept it along with many others in a locked drawer of his old desk – it was not to be defaced by trite suggestions of 'prophetic'. She saw these roses – white, red – like kind but agonizing clenched fists raging with demented compassion. Gareth was a night-rose, as she, and many others were too. Sometimes she felt almost as if she had counted them all, one by one, counting casualties as insomniacs count sheep.

She coughed on a cigarette as she craned out of her living room window at the spot where the lane bent round towards the turn-off from the main road. Christopher was a few minutes late. She pushed herself between a sideboard and the bay of the window and waited for the sight of his car's snout as it turned the corner under the dark interwoven spread of the branches of wintry trees. Even from that distance she could tell the branches were still dripping after the early rain. She knew her house, and the trees immediately around it, the way an expert knows his chosen subject. There were no people in that knowledge other than Christopher. Her clothes were carelessly chosen. She did not wear them to look attractive. They were loose clothes, indeterminate middle- and late-twentieth-century clothes. These clothes she had worn for years, the cigarette she always had in her hand or dangling from her lips, made her look incompetent, perpetually shaken and as if dowdiness had been chosen as her only suitable appearance.

No one used the lane except on week days. There was the butcher's van, the grocer's van, the baker's van, the fishmonger's van once a fortnight, and the coal-merchant's lorry once a month. Each brought and delivered her small, thrifty orders. Christopher's car squeezed over these previous runnels in the February mud. He waved before he got out, as he always did, and she went from the window to the front door. It always happened that the sound of the door opening coincided with the slam of the car door closing. A careful man, Christopher watched his shoes on the muddy path from which the gravel had long been washed away. Harriet came down one welcoming pace on the doorstep, because – it is a paraphrase of a love poem – you go forwards to those you love although as you wait for them it seems they have a greater distance to cover before they reach you. She took pleasure in affirming the meanings of her husband's poems.

As soon as they were inside, Harriet went to the kitchen to supervise their Sunday lunch. Christopher hung his coat in the hall and after saying things about traffic and weather went into the living room. Every time he went in there the room and its furniture met him with the force of a small shock. The room never changed. It was the same mixture of everything in its place and slow dilapidation. Wear and tear were more conspicuous than familiarity. Breathing its air was a different sensation from anything he had known in any other room he had been in. The room was specific; it was as particular as the right answer in a lengthy calculation. He said, through the open door, 'Do you still have my old rocking-horse?'

He waited for an answer, hearing a pot lid rattled on the work-surface by the sink. He went over to the window and looked out at the small, untended lawn now smeared with winter, where he had spent years playing under his mother's eye. Harriet appeared at the living room door in an apron and with an oven-glove on one hand. 'Of course, I still have it. Why do you ask?'

'They've become trendy,' he explained. 'A man I met during the week was saying they fetch a small fortune in the antique trade.'

'Trendy?' she asked.

'Going with the trend. Up to the latest fashion.'

'Oh, I see. But you don't want to sell ours?'

'I thought it might interest you,' he humoured.

She shrugged. 'I suppose it does.' She went back to the kitchen and Christopher followed. 'What's wrong with new ones? Don't they make them any longer?'

'I've no idea.'

'Then don't suggest I should sell ours. You know why.'

'I wasn't,' he said. 'Absolutely not.'

Warmed by the old Aga, they sat eating Sunday lunch in the kitchen. Since his mid-twenties, with his growing salary, Christopher had been bringing a bottle of wine on his Sunday visits. It added the encouragement Harriet needed to make Sunday into more of an occasion. It didn't show in her dress though it reflected in how lunch itself was served, on wedding-present china on a white tablecloth instead of the waxed gingham patterned kitchen table-covering rubbed away to the canvas on each corner and in crosses where it had been folded too often.

'Another new suit?' she asked.

'Why not?' he said, defending himself with a widening smile.

'You're becoming quite the dandy . . .'

'A large wardrobe impresses the clients. Theirs, of course, are supposed to impress *me*.'

Harriet enjoyed the moving pictures in her mind in which men like film stars of the late 1930s and early 1940s vied with each other in a competition of sartorial elegance. It was a world she had virtually forgotten and it amused her to think that Christopher starred in its latest version of fashion.

'How about Hayward's widow? Any developments there?'

'None,' said Harriet, seriously. 'I'm *adamant*. And they won't find me giving in. You won't see *me* going on television.' It was what Christopher expected to hear. Always, though, in spite of being prepared for it, that tone of bitterness, edged fuzzily in her voice, disturbed him enough to make him back down from a subject he did not want to leave alone. 'I won't be that kind of a representative of the dead.'

'You're probably right,' Christopher said slowly. 'You should do what you think best.' He had always found it difficult to talk to his mother on any subject connected with his father or his father's poetry. Harriet either clamped up in morose hostility or told him severely to talk about something else. 'You ought to be pleased with the interest they're showing . . .' He hesitated on this unfamiliar ground. 'You should be, you know.'

'I'm neither pleased or displeased,' his mother said. From the way Harriet looked at him, Christopher could sense she was asking herself what his motive was for raising questions which he, more than anyone else, knew she did not like to hear. When he turned round to face her, after putting their plates in the sink, she said, 'Do you know what I wish they'd stop doing? I wish they'd not keep on saying, "What kind of poet would he have become *if* . . .?" It was more of her own thoughts on Gareth Mortimer than she was in the habit of saying, even to her son.

'Perhaps you ought not to read what these people write about him.'

'Florence Hayward keeps *sending* me these things,' and Harriet was almost irate in the way she suggested she didn't want the cuttings and reviews and publications that arrived in the post from Roger Hayward's widow. 'She probably *knows* I don't like Roger Hayward's work. I think his poems are brutal. He wrote like someone who was actually *glad* to be in a war.'

'They say authors often don't read the reviews of their books. Perhaps their widows ought to do the same.'

Harriet began to show signs of her customary reluctance to speak of herself and the parsimonious way she had administered Gareth Mortimer's literary estate. She was surprised, and worried, that Christopher should suddenly start to take more of an interest in it. His casual tone of voice took her by surprise, too. It was a long way from his respectful silences of the past.

'The most I'll admit to,' said Harriet, announcing that this was the end of what she would say on the subject, 'is disappointment – disappointment in people preferring Roger Hayward's poems to your father's.'

'You haven't helped by refusing to co-operate, though, have you?'

'I've given them permission to use his poems.'

'What about the unpublished ones you won't let *anyone* see? Or his letters? His manuscripts?'

'Why should I? They're mine. They're even *about* me.'

'Shall I do the dishes?' he asked.

'Why, all of a sudden, are you so interested in your father's poetry?'

'I don't know.' They looked at each other in silence. 'It's you,' he said.

'Me?'

'It seems mean.'

'Only because you don't understand.'

'I was re-reading them the other night. Engineers do read sometimes, you know. And you're right. My father's poems are totally different from Hayward's.'

'Everyone *says* they're different. The 'trend', however,' she sneered, 'is for cruelty. Hayward was a poetic gangster.'

'And it's because they're different you've refused to co-operate in their programme . . .'

'Christopher, it's *my business*,' she protested. 'I've devoted my life to what's best for your father's work.'

'And what's best for any writer's work, surely, is publication . . .'

'They have *enough*.'

'. . . of *all* of it.'

'I'm only possessive of what's *mine*.'

'And I'm his son,' he said quietly, finding it hard to believe he had drawn his mother as far as he had without the subtle probing he had felt would have been necessary.

'You're my son, too.' Christopher nodded, taking back most of what he'd said before. 'And you'll admit it yourself, you're hardly an expert in poetry let alone his. You must leave me to look after what I know most about.'

Christopher knew how difficult it was for him to think of himself as Gareth Mortimer's son. He had never seen his father and his father had never seen him. He was like a biological memory. Or a story his mother told him when he was a child and which he could never quite forget. His father seemed fictitious. He was a resented absentee, who'd left printed relics. He'd left behind more than love, but things – not objects exactly, but words, things made of words – in which he was preserved, his voiceprint pickled in print.

'They've asked *you*,' his mother said to his back, as he stood before the sink, his hands in water, 'to go on that programme.'

'How did you know?'

'*I guessed.*'

'You know I won't if you don't want me to.'

'You promise you won't do it?'

'Yes. I promise.'

'Good.'

'What good would I be anyway? It's not as if I know very much about him.'

'And they don't either.'

'When I was at school, I tried to boast about him. They hadn't even heard of him. What really cut a dash was that my father had been killed in the war. The fact that he had, so to speak, written about his own death before it happened, was of no distinction whatsoever.'

Harriet sent him way from the sink. He went into the living room and sat down as the clouds cleared patchily from the sky and the wind blew harder through the trees that surrounded Harriet's house. He was glad his mother had refused to have anything to do with the programme Hayward's widow had pestered a producer into undertaking. Apart from whatever dignity there is in refusing to publicize yourself, Harriet's grief, her glamourless devotion, were ill-suited to any kind of exposure. He could hardly understand it himself. He remembered all the times he had seen her working at his father's desk. Papers had been left in it and others had been returned by the Army. She had scrutinized each sheet a thousand times. It was a composite memory in which he was various young ages while each picture that flicked through it came with a glint of weather and various shades of daylight and dusk. 'Mummy's busy,' she'd say if he interrupted her. 'What are you writing?' he'd ask. 'A book,' Harriet would say. 'I'm writing a book about your father.' For all he knew now, she was still writing it. She would always be writing it. How could a man who had been dead for so long continue to cause such trouble?

> *Imaginary o'clock, time for the dead*
> *To laugh their heads off in infinity*
> *Where, hiding out, they're really in your head . . .*

Even Christopher had his father's lines stuck in his brain like neural pests. As a child he had known well enough that his father was a poet. Harriet had proudly shown him his books. People had thought him famous enough to visit Harriet and ask questions. They were coolly received, given tea, told nothing, and sent away. She was more self-confident then in her customary loose suits and carelessly groomed hair. When he first read Gareth Mortimer's two thin books he hadn't understood a word. They were so thin, hardly like real books at all. Harriet gave him copies of his own on his sixteenth birthday and when he was at university someone had published the *Collected Poems*. Gareth Mortimer's publisher lost patience with Harriet's delays, which had become increasingly short-tempered. He commissioned a young critic and poet to do the best he could, and, though Harriet had seen him a few times, their meetings had been far from placid. It was a mis-named volume which its editor introduced by lamenting the 'improbable possessiveness' of a woman he named as 'Gareth's widow'. Harriet was infuriated by a usage of her husband's first name which she couldn't be persuaded to accept as a literary convention. 'He didn't *know* him,' she shouted. 'He was only nine when your father died,' she said to her son.

Christopher stood up and sighed as these memories ended. He went into his mother's room. Something of his father was in him;

but he had no means of identifying it. On his father's desk were diaries, notebooks, papers, letters and poems – materials of Harriet's book, the book she might never finish. Other papers were neatly filed in thin folders on the shelves of the two bookcases with locked glass doors which also preserved his father's library. This time he stood back from the desk and looked at it without disturbing any of the relics that lay on its surface or were hidden in its drawers. He knew what was there – pens, ink bottles, unused sheets of paper; a pair of gloves, and a cigarette-box with a broken clasp and a box of matches more than three decades old, one of which he'd struck when he was about fourteen and then held until the experimental fire burned his finger; gum, a toothbrush for cleaning his typewriter, pencils, envelopes, postage stamps, that, like the old coins there – big, brown pennies, solid threepenny-bits – were of another age; and a photograph of Harriet, twenty-one years old. She slept in sight of these things in the desk. Gareth Mortimer had never seen that room. He'd never been in it. He'd never seen the house or known it existed, though Christopher had thought that if his father had seen it, then he would have known what it was his poems prophesied. Harriet curated the room like an exhibit in the house where the poet had worked, looking out, season by season, into the bedraggled ranks of birch trees. Her room did not seem to be in 1978 but farther back in the era she lived in. It was a summery wartime when spirits were high. Christopher could not *see* 1940, or 1941, or 1942, or any of these years. Yet he felt them present in Harriet's house and they were like shy pets that take to corners when strangers come in.

They sat in the living room. Coffee dregs were cold in their cups. A clock in its wooden case tocked as if determined to unwind itself as quickly as it could into a dead stop of sudden quiet that would reveal everything they were unable to say to each other. Ash collapsed in the grate; hot powders shifted in glows and the fire drew back into its embers and vanished in grey as if the light had been exhausted in them. It was like all their winter Sundays, that moment. It grew darker outside, bit by bit, in sudden stages instead of smoothly. Harriet threw her smoked stubs into the fire, one by one.

'With what you two have in common,' Christopher said, 'it strikes me as inevitable that you'll meet' – and he paused before the name – 'Florence Hayward. Without her, you'd be unique.'

'If she so much as knocked on my door,' Harriet said with a scowl on her lips, 'I wouldn't let her in.'

Firelight – what was left of it – blotched Harriet's face as she sat back in her chair. She slid into the growing darkness of the room. It was a reply of sorts, and it silenced Christopher, who, after a few moments, said, 'Is there anything you need?'

'No.'

'I'll have someone rewire the place in the spring. It's high time. You know, I worry about you out here miles from nowhere and the fire brigade and with this old-fashioned wiring.' He couldn't see his mother's face. 'You were lucky to miss a burst pipe this winter.'

'So practical, Christopher,' she said, almost laughing. 'I don't understand how you could have turned out to be so practical.'

'Yes. I know. Unlike my father. Unpoetical,' he said with a tone of resignation.

'The publisher says I *should*,' she said. 'He says I've a responsibility to *him*. If I prepare a bigger edition then it will sell more and help Gareth. And he says I haven't been helpful so far, have I? It's only fair to come clean *now*, he says. What does he mean by 'now'? That I should have forgotten him anyway? I don't know what to do.' Everyone involved in her dilemma seemed to have been dismissed – Christopher, Florence Hayward, editors, publishers, producers – everyone except Gareth. 'You know,' she confided, leaning into what light was left in the fire, 'I've been so faithful. I've never known a man since, and I never knew one before. But they don't understand.'

Despite his embarrassment, Christopher was eager to hear more of his mother's desperate fidelity. He had always known it, but attached no significance to it. But she withdrew into the dark again as if she had already said too much. 'There are poems they've never seen,' she said, from the darkness on the other side of the firelight. 'Poems he wrote and never printed. He showed me everything he wrote. Or he sent them to me when he was away. I can hardly believe he wrote so much in such a short time. There are more poems in my room than there are in the *Collected Poems*. Better poems, too. There were half a dozen that arrived after he was dead. He never saw you, but he wrote about you, too. You, me, and your father . . . Why do other people want them? They have nothing to do with them. They're mine. Private things.'

'Well, as you know, I don't really have a taste in poetry . . .'

'Don't you think they'd leave me in peace? *They* think of me as a quaint, eccentric little widow who can't bear to let her love letters out of her sight.'

He had never realized before how forcefully she detested anyone other than herself who had an interest in Gareth Mortimer's poems. She hated anyone who had ever read them. In the silence that followed, four lines Christopher knew by heart went through his mind.

A choir of widows hired a hall
To sing to their new sisters.
Their lovely songs could not console
Eavesdropping widowers.

They made him feel like a widower.

'Harriet, dear Harriet,' said Harriet, mimicking a letter from Hayward's widow, 'do, please, send me a chapter of your book. I'm so looking forward to reading about your life with Gareth, and written by *you*, who, like me, was so lucky to have met and married one of the finest poets of our time.' She paused, breathless with the venom of how she had delivered her impersonation of a woman she had never heard speak. 'But she's *different*.'

'I haven't read her book,' said Christopher.

'Oh, do, *please*. It will show you *exactly* what I mean. There's no love in it.'

'Mother, she remarried . . . She's, well . . . temperamentally, she *is* different. She isn't even called Hayward any more.'

'It's how she signs her letters to *me*.'

'Is it?'

'And it's how she signed her introduction to Roger Hayward's *Collected Poems* with the frontispiece and footnotes. And *her* book.'

'She hadn't remarried by then.'

'All and sundry who ever wanted to rummage through Roger Hayward's papers have been given *carte blanche*. She even,' Harriet cried with disbelief, 'sold them to a *library* for a very fat sum. Anyone who wants to read Hayward's papers has to go to Texas, for God's sake. Texas!'

'I know what's in father's desk . . .'

'You were *meant* to look.'

'That stuff's better not kept, surely . . . It's – well, it *is* morbid.'

'They'll get nothing from me,' Harriet said. He knew that even if Harriet wanted to appear personally on that programme, or introduce a new, full edition of Gareth Mortimer's poems, she couldn't. Something like a promise she had made years ago stood in her way. To go against it now would turn her life into a mistake, or a lie.

Christopher leaned over to the fire and poked it. He placed small kindling over what promising coals survived in it. When that lit and began to burn he put a larger piece of wood on top. 'It's hardly normal,' he said. 'You're denying those who have a legitimate and probably quite enthusiastic interest in his work.'

'They can have what they like when I'm dead.'

'That's hardly a very helpful way of looking at it. By then I'll be the one who decides, and I'll always want to do what you'd have done.'

'Your father's is the only important poetic output over which someone who loved him has complete control. If it had been up to him, *he* would have published it, of course. But it isn't. It's up to *me*.'

'I don't know anything about poetry,' Christopher said, as, with an old-fashioned pair of tongs, he placed small pieces of coal on the brightening fire. For several minutes more he raked in the bucket by the hearth for suitably sized larger pieces and then worked them into the burning design he was artificing out of black coal and flame. He sat back again, rubbing his hands. 'You know I don't like driving in the dark,' he said.

'Do you want some tea before you go?'

'I'd better make a start.'

'I'd like you to hear something first.'

Christopher hesitated. 'You may have said too much already.'

'Gareth met Hayward. Only once. They didn't like each other. Hayward mentions it in his journal. She printed it in her book. Well, she's a liar. She's worse than that. She's a fraud. Gareth wrote to me. He said Hayward told him he'd been unfaithful to her, and she to him. She was living with someone else. And Hayward knew it. He didn't even mind. You see, they weren't like us. They were nothing like Gareth and me. But she wrote very little of *that* sort.'

Harriet got up and went through to her room. A few seconds of being alone in the living room forced Christopher to get on his feet and do something. He switched on a lamp, one that stood near the window. Harriet, he knew, hated bright lights. He was drawing the curtains when she came back.

She sat down and opened a folder. It lay on her lap showing sheets of paper, some handwritten, others typewritten. 'He wrote this on the day he heard Hayward had been killed.' He heard his mother laugh under her breath. It was a laugh no one was meant to hear, one that people keep for the recognition of ironies which, for some reason, are usually detected in private. 'If I edited an edition with notes, with chunks quoted out of letters, this would do Florence Hayward no good at all. Hayward didn't mind, you know. He was just as unfaithful. He was quite famous in the war years. He said in his journal that he found Gareth 'tedious'.'

'Can I see it?'

Harriet shook her head.

'Then why produce whatever it is . . .? I'm not really interested in their marriage.'

Harriet read the poem aloud.

Her infidelities have been confirmed,
Though he, who's been unfaithful, won't complain
Of tittle-tattle in the mess, where, warmed
On Scotch-and-soda, staring at the rain
He sees our regimental roses die
In the storm-winds of autumn. 'Talk to me,'
He says, then says, 'The rule of verse is – lie;
Then try to get away with it. History –
Now that's a harder game.' I like verse sweet
And in its sweetness doomed to speak the truth
Of how we feel when our two bodies meet
Mysteriously confused by love and youth.

But that was years ago, another life.
Then we had words like love, son, and wife.
Now there is nothing. Could she understand
That ringless finger on his severed hand?

'Perhaps,' said Christopher, 'it would be an idea if you were to read me his poems more often.'

'One day,' she said, 'I'd like to hear *you* read them.'

He felt himself tall, unmarried in an expensive coat and a man who was about to return to his apartment along a smooth motorway. He felt himself to be a successful, unheroic representative of the late 1970s, as much as his father had been characteristic of the casualties of a war, and whose voice, in his poems, whispered its spokesmanship on behalf of the dead – that poet of absences, of civilian memories confronting him in military depots, during training routines, on landing-ships, on battlefields.

'You never knew me,' she said, 'when I was happy.' It sounded as if Harriet spoke from far away in a place where'd she lived before he was born.

'Why did you do it?'

'And I'll keep on doing it,' Harriet said, in the same voice. 'I can't bear the thought of not being in love with him.' She laughed her under-her-breath laugh, a series of arrested breaths. 'For all I know that might be how Florence Hayward feels too, except that she doesn't possess the habit of honesty. Are you sure you can't stay?' she asked, like a girlfriend.

'I'll stay next week. It's the best I can do,' he added, to her upturned face. 'I don't like to think of you living here on your own . . . Letting the fire go out, practically in the dark with all those books and papers on your lap. You let the house get too cold sometimes.' He looked at his watch. It was new. She hadn't seen it before. She looked up at him approvingly. 'I'd better go then.'

'Fifty miles,' she said.

'Yes.' He smiled. 'I can do it in an hour, quite easily.'

Harriet walked with her son to his car. The raggedy front lawn was yellowed by electric light from the open door. Harriet waved him off, thinking – it was a paraphrase of a love poem – that when someone left, it seemed you walked more than half the way with him, except that in the poem it was 'her'.

THE EARL OF HELL'S WAISTCOAT

Augusta Boswell didn't think of herself as a lucky woman. So when she opened a book in the secondhand dealer's in Edinburgh and saw clearly that it had come from the library of the only man with whom she had ever been in love, her feelings were those of good fortune modified by heart-rending surprise.

It was twenty years since she had last seen Erskine Gibb Geddes's elaborate bookplate. At one time it had been familiar from scores of books borrowed or consulted in his rooms in the Cambridge college where he'd been a Fellow. From early in the eighteenth century his family had enjoyed increasing mercantile success in Dundee. Around 1910 these interests had been sold off. Erskine Gibb Geddes's branch of the family settled into a gentrified life in Perthshire. Others emigrated to ranches in Montana and Texas or to pastoral properties in New South Wales. Trade was celebrated on the engraved bookplate by a two-masted vessel, perhaps too fancifully galleon-like to be taken seriously, with a pile of books on the right-hand side, and the façade of the Geddes's family house on the other. It had been engraved to Erskine's brief by Joan Hassall as far back as 1947 when he was ten – 'The best birthday present I ever had,' was how he'd referred to it.

The book was Eve Blantyre Simpson's *Folklore in Lowland Scotland.* As well as Erskine's bookplate there were marginalia, endpaper annotations in his small, neat, scholarly and still perfectly legible pencilled handwriting. The bookplate jolted her. Notes in his own hand, however, intensified the recognition and she felt momentarily enfeebled and drained. She held the book against her and supported herself against the shelves with her other hand. She was the only customer in that part of the shop, and out of sight of the proprietor. She wiped an eye with a handkerchief and let the effects of sorrowful serendipity – its griefs and pleasures – wear off.

'Do you, by any chance, have others? With this bookplate?' she asked the proprietor's back. 'Mr Hogarth, have you more where this came from, please?'

'Oh, Dr Boswell. Nice day again,' he said, waving his arms in an apology of absentmindedness. 'You caught me in a deep dwam.' It was hard to tell if his impression of being busily preoccupied elsewhere was a genuine reflection of bookish concentration or a ploy calculated to disguise his financial interest in his stock. He looked at the bookplate. 'Delightful. Worth having for the plate alone,' he said.

'But did you acquire any more from the same source?' She was impatient. Although considered an academic oddity at five feet tall in any of her large selection of brogue shoes, tweed two-pieces and symbolic Celtic jewellery, Dr Boswell was known equally for her forthright manner. 'Do you have *others?*'

'I have.'

'I'll take them.'

'There's rather a lot,' Hogarth said on a rippling laugh that was supposed to make Dr Boswell say, 'How many?' with a shudder at the possible cost.

'Work out a price. Ring me at my department. If I'm not there leave a note of the sum with my secretary.'

'It'll take a wee while, that will,' an assistant said with thin-voiced disbelief.

'Are you sure you're not being . . . a bit impulsive, Dr Boswell?'

'Quite sure.'

'We're talking three, four hundred vols here. Some very tasty items. Not a few rarities. I gave a decent price, to, I believe, the sister of the deceased. Are you quite sure?' Hogarth asked in his slow, sly tones.

'And if I'm buying the rest, then I don't suppose you'll mind if I take this with me?'

'Oh, well, if you're sure, then I suppose so,' Hogarth said grudgingly.

'A very carnaptious wee woman,' Hogarth said to the young man, who was also his son, although it's doubtful if even regular customers knew of the relationship.

'A really cracking sale. One fell swoop!'

'Dr *Augusta* Boswell!'

'I look forward to seeing her signature on a cheque!'

'That toxic wee spinster's *loaded*. And one day, there's every chance her executors will bear the firm of Hogarth in mind after she's kicked off her clogs, son. Then they'll come back,' he said lyrically. 'Well, let's get weaving! Sooner packed, soonest paid for.'

'What about the price, Dad?'

'Ach, you think of a figure. Go on, say a sum, son.'

'One thousand five hundred!' the son shouted triumphantly.

'Och, away! Nearer four! Let's say 3,685.'

'What did you pay for them?'

'Money and fair words!'

When Augusta Boswell first met Erskine Gibb Geddes in 1961 she'd just come down from St Andrews to Cambridge to do her doctorate. Erskine, who'd completed his only two years before, was assigned as her supervisor. He was twenty-eight; she was twenty-one. She was diminutive, brilliant, dotty and charming; he was lanky, thin, already with a slight stoop, ascetic, an elegant, scholarly recluse, pale, fair-haired, inward and melancholy. What they had in common was means – New Town old wealth behind Augusta Boswell, lapsed Dundonian commerce turned into estates and serious finance (about which he need never concern himself) bolstering Erskine Gibb Geddes's bibliographical demands on life. They were two of a kind. They shared a devotion to the early history of Britain, Arthurian legends, early literatures and languages, druidism, the fairy faith of the Celtic lands, folklore and archaeology. From each animated, industrious, successful and sometimes ruthless family had emerged a gentle scholar for whom getting and spending meant nothing at all. On Augusta's side of the matter it was love at first sight.

But for a woman as lively as Augusta was in her younger years Erskine's apparent frailty and obsessive study made it hard going.

'You're not *just* my supervisor. We're friends, too, aren't we?'

'I wish you'd put this to one side, instead of pressing me with it.' He spoke slowly and carefully.

'Why are you so opposed to coming with me on my field trip?'

'Irregularities of that sort are usually found out. One way or another the culprits are discovered.'

''Culprits?' I'm not suggesting anything criminal.'

'I have my book to finish.'

'Is it possible that you're scared to cross the walls of the college for fear of the outside world?'

'Nonsense!'

'You hardly *ever* go *anywhere*, Erskine!'

'Then, yes, if one has an ivory tower, one tends to prefer it.'

'I don't just 'admire your mind'.'

'Well, I admire yours. Your work is outstanding.'

'I think you're as fond of me as I am of you, but you can't say or do anything about it. Erskine, we're two extremely fortunate people. Youth, money, talent . . . Why do you have to define yourself as monastic and saintly?'

He turned to look at her for the first time in that conversation. 'I think I'm frightened of being found out.'

'I don't understand,' she said, scared on her own account in case of what he might say next.

'I think it's to do with money. I've no idea what I'm worth, but also, I've never experienced want. I was considered too delicate for school and educated privately. I don't know much about 'out there'. I'm not just shy and timid. I've never known desire.'

'And for me? What do you feel for me?'

'Affection. Interest. Concern. Admiration.' He said these words with difficulty, pausing between them, then turning his head away once more, as if distracted by the shrub that wavered in the wind outside his window.

'Are you homosexual?'

'No, Augusta,' he said quietly. 'I'm not.'

Hogarth could have asked three times as much and Augusta Boswell would have paid it. Her inherited house, and its inherited furniture and inherited pictures, were backed up by invisible, inherited wherewithal.

Surrounded by those of Erskine Gibb Geddes's books which his sister had sold to Hogarth, Augusta found herself in a more unsettling dimension of the past than she had experienced before. It was different from her memories of their times together, especially that first summer trip which he'd come round to sharing with her. Trains and buses appalled him. Sensitive, unworldly, and coddled, he was terrified of ordinary life. They'd travelled to a score of different, interesting sites, in a Rolls-Royce hired complete with driver. They looked an unusual couple leaving a Rolls-Royce dressed for walking, she in shorts, each with a light rucksack and heavy hiking boots, as they set out for places associated with lore and legend. She sketched, photographed and took notes, while he spouted erudition in full flight like a man released from years of self-confinement in which silence and tutorial whispers were the only events. 'I know what you are,' she remembered him saying, as if the phrase took weeks to put together. 'You're a *scamp* of scholarship.'

'It's not quite how I think of myself. It must be my height.'

She remembered, too, the moment when he said, 'Should we try kissing?' and how she said, 'I knew I was right to wait until *you* asked. It didn't take as long as I thought.'

A week later – she was lightly amused as well as happy – he realized that he'd discovered want and desire. Weeks later, in his rooms in Cambridge, he said, 'Love-making isn't the least bit 'literary', is it? Or do you think so?'

'Is it meant to be? Just because numberless poets have gone on about it in countless rhapsodies doesn't make it 'literary'. My father didn't have a 'literary' bone in his body, nor my mother, but they managed to produce me. Did you want it to be 'literary'?'

'I like it a lot, but there's an animal absurdity to it which really does puzzle me when I think about how poetic it's supposed to be.'

On another occasion: 'Not a lot goes on here without certain Fellows getting wind of it,' he said. 'I don't foresee a scandal, but it could be mentioned, and I'd be expected to do something about it.'

'Such as?'

'Resign my Fellowship.'

'Would you?'

'I wouldn't like that. Why don't you move into a flat or a house? Then we could be together more often, and propriety would be served as far as here's concerned.'

But faced with piles of Erskine's books wasn't the same as remembering him. The sensation was different. He'd died too long ago for her grief to be unbearable. There were days and nights to remember, pleasant things, which, if the hopes in them had been dashed in the mid-1960s, were enough to remind her that the person she'd become was not the person she was before. But his books . . . They were objects of his life, and more meaningful than her gorgeously expensive engagement ring and two brooches, a silk scarf and his British Museum library ticket, or the receipt for a room in a Bloomsbury hotel where they'd spent four nights in 1964. She'd read many of these books and possessed many of them in her own library; but they competed strangely with her treasured relics – two brooches still worn, as well as the Jacqmar silk scarf – and stood on a plane of significance similar to Erskine's letters to her, even the last few dozen of them. They were more secretive, but of her own past, too, where the language now seemed different and the realm in which they'd lived seemed to have a different name. They were from the time of her body. Looking at his handwritten marginalia, his notes on fly-leaves and endpapers, felt like a discovery of the truths that lurked in what she'd forgotten, or misremembered. Or else she'd altered them in the intimacy of time as she pursued a desperate need to keep the past vivid and alive.

Each evening when she returned from the university she devoted herself to compiling a coherent summary of Erskine's notes and marginalia. They were in a more personal, more subjective, more candid style than that of his only publication. *Pre-Christian Faiths and Beliefs in Northern Europe*, the foundations for which had been his doctoral thesis, had become something like an acknowledged major work by 1990, but the reviews after its appearance in 1967 – it was in keeping with

Erskine's luck that it should finally come out eight months after his death – had been contentious, nit-pickingly pedantic, and, in their last paragraphs, dismissive. Old-guard scholars, deep in retirement, on the verge of it, or half-dead, lashed out at the innovative and original.

But other things had been noted in Erskine's books, too. In several volumes he'd copied a folk rhyme. They were all dated 1965, when he was ill, and had moved back to the house in Perthshire, the house whose façade was engraved on his bookplate. It was

I stood upon Eyemouth fort,
And guess ye what I saw?
Fernieside and Flemington
Newhouses and Cocklaw;
The fairy fouk o' Fosterland,
The witches o' Edincraw,
The bogle-bo o' Billy Myre,
Wha kills our bairns a'.

It would have read as a routine and undisturbing memorandum had he not repeated it in several books, and had he not underlined the last two lines, and had the date been earlier than 1965, when he knew that he was a dying man. They had spoken of having children. She detested the idea of her family being continued by cousins for whose crass ambitions in law, politics and high finance she had nothing but contempt. At first, the thought of paternity filled Erskine with terror; but then, before he met Augusta Boswell, before she changed his life, the idea of love reduced him to elegant stuttering and lassitude. She was in two minds about her influence on his life. Had he never met her, had she suffered love in timid solitude, would he have been alive still? Had he, by nature, by something more profound than mere temperament, been chosen for a life of scholarly solitariness, which she, intrusively, and fatally, had shattered with passion and love? Or was that bairn-killing bogle-bo merely a metaphor for disease, death, and the sundering of all contentments and futures before they could cross from dreams to reality?

The bogle-bo o' Billy Myre,
Wha kills our bairns a'.

It was how he tended to read folk poetry; but she was unconvinced. Or, rather, it was how she, too, read folk poetry, but not that particular poem.

When they were lovers, but before marriage and children entered their conversations and prospects, she'd felt contempt and consternation for Erskine's self-pitying remorse for his substantial but indefinable wealth. It seemed to pollute him, as if he lived in a vision in which his unearned circumstances existed in constant contrast with the poverty, hardships and deprivation of so many others. 'I am very wealthy,' she said. She was naked at the time and half-sitting on her desk in the bedroom of her flat. 'Indeed, I've inherited a fortune. You, too, are very wealthy. Indeed, you've inherited a fortune, too, perhaps of the more nebulous, less discloseable kind than my own, but a great, a very great, deal. So, I have a fortune, and you have a fortune. To you this is a state of affairs which promises absolute misery.' He tried to interrupt but Augusta would have none of it. 'Do you know a single don in your college, or my college, or *any* college, in Cambridge, or Oxford, or in *any* university, who wouldn't give his or her eye teeth for a *fraction* our our combined resources?'

'Oh, well, I mean, if you put it like that . . . I . . . well . . . No, I . . .'

'I've seen poor people. They don't deserve it, no more than we deserve to be rich. But, *I can't help it, and neither can you.*' She was sure the memory was accurate; she was certain she was trying to recall the episode with total honesty and clarity. All the same, she wondered if she'd taken advantage of his quiet, broken, pusillanimous temperament. Or was she overstating to herself now how fierce, forthright and scornful she was with him? 'I'm like you. I'm just like you in some ways. I'm frightened of what I've got, who I am, and of how what I've got makes me who I am, to even *want* to be political. I back out of it. I tell myself the world's got nothing to do with me. There are times when I actually believe I'm above all that mess and noise, all that chasing about in search of money, or something to eat, or amusement, or whatever . . . But I'm not above it. I like to think I am, but I'm not.'

How long did it take for them to get round to talking about the future and what they could do in a life together? Timescales concertina'd in her mind. No sooner did she remember one significant incident and what was said than it seemed that the next, the step forward, happened a few minutes later, when she knew it took weeks, or months. So – 'What I find myself imagining,' he said, 'is *independent* scholarship. We could live at Lindorack. Of course, from the point of view of publication, and reputation, a university post is very much to be desired. How about you? Do you have your mind set on a university career? Have you dreamt of the crowning glory of a Chair?'

'I know Lindorack's yours. But what about your sister, who lives there?' she asked.

'You don't know Daphne very well. But I think you know enough to feel that she wouldn't be any trouble. Well, yes . . . Actually, Daphne's part of what's been on my mind. Marriage appears to be very low on her list of priorities. She seems interested only in running the estate – and in her painting. She likes you. She'd be delighted if we populated the place with little Geddeses.'

'I'd like that, too.'

'But there's your thesis, and your book.'

'Am I planning to write a book?'

'Your research is too good not to!'

'I can write it at Lindorack.'

'You've about a year's work to finish. And you can't go anywhere until you've completed it,' he said.

Other rhymes and poems on the endpapers and flyleaves of his books were, she decided, of his own composition.

It is dark. It is very dark.
Black as the Earl of Hell's waistcoat.
Dark, dark as opposite. Dark as the is-not.

That, too, was dated in the months of his dying. He'd always been in the habit of saying things like, 'Talk about blank? Talk about there being nothing in the stupid man's mind! It must be as black as the Earl of Hell's waistcoat in there.' She'd forgotten that. It came back with a jolt. All these years of remembering and that tic-simile hadn't once got through!

Her library overlooked the square. The electric pale green of the trees didn't witness her reading-lamp go out until long after revellers had passed by with their shouts and laughter.

Let love accumulate, more, more, and more,
And ours be happy children and delight,

she read on a flyleaf. As poetry it was probably poor, old-fashioned stuff, but she was agreeably hurt that Erskine had tried to write it, even at a time when the imperative of his heart-felt sentiment was utterly without hope – the date showed that. But after all those years weeping was impossible, with or without another glass from a second bottle of Sauternes. 'Is that really true, Augusta? Sweet wines are 'unfashionable'?'

'I read it in a newspaper last Sunday.'

'But dry wines don't taste as nice!' he protested.

'Hedonism isn't supposed to be you.'

'All right with fish, I suppose, but . . .'

'My theory is that dry wine is a puritanical reflex in a pleasure-seeking decade.'

It was at her bedroom window at around 3 a.m. that August night that Augusta Boswell became a nocturnal person and discovered the sad pleasures of the moon. The long, walled garden behind her house was adequately looked after by a Mr Paterson, whom she rarely saw or thought about and who was paid every Friday by Mrs McLennan, who did the housework three days a week. Balmy weather, a clear and starry sky, and the moon, with only the faintest rustle of leaves, drew her to go outside. She took her bottle of wine, put on a hat from a peg by the kitchen door, and took a large torch from a drawer.

For several minutes she stared at the sky's astral remoteness, its lunar immensity, its universal, dwarfing scale that humbled whoever contemplated it while comforting the observer's loneliness. She felt alone with the grandeur of time, to which every life that is or ever was adds a pathetic pittance. She sat down on a chair by a garden table. It wasn't bright enough to read. Flowers were almost colourless, trees grey-green. It felt like a personal outdoors although overlooked by other houses. At that hour almost all were in darkness save for a few hall lights and some in which late parties were still in full swing. They were far enough away to be silent. People had come home from late performances accompanied by friends, strangers and artists of one kind or another. From the unlit window of a bedroom in a high flat a man was rapidly dressing when he noticed a tiny woman in a broad-brimmed hat apparently moonbathing. In another flat a woman had dashed into a room to find the text of a play in order to illustrate once and for all the hideous deviations perpetrated by a director, who, in the sitting room, was defending his integrity to a dozen people as well oiled as himself. She switched the light off and looked out. She saw a small woman in a towelling bath-robe and wide-brimmed hat holding a torch on a book. Or that it is what she decided she saw after a good two minutes of scrutinizing the unnerving nocturnal vagueness of the sight. A hand reached out for a glass that sat beside a bottle on a table.

On a dozen consecutive nights after that, at approximately the same time, the same woman excused herself from her guests to look out of the high window. She saw the same woman in the wide-brimmed hat. On the third night the lighting arrangements had clearly been improved by the introduction of a desk lamp led from the kitchen on an extended cable. There was a pile of books, a bottle, a glass, and sometimes the woman wrote on a pad. She didn't mention it to her guests. More than once the woman at the garden table appeared only to be basking in the moonlight in that uncharacteristically sustained run of fine weather.

But Dr Boswell was hard at work. She'd decided that *Pre-Christian Faiths and Beliefs in Northern Europe* was due for a revision only she could perform. She was drafting a chapter in the form of an appendix in which Erskine's marginalia and other notes would be interpreted. Daphne Geddes had been written to seeking her permission and asking for her help. Augusta also asked why she'd sold her brother's books, if she'd sold all of them, and if his notebooks and other papers were still at Lindorack.

Three months before he died, Augusta moved in to Lindorack to help Daphne with nursing and caring for Erskine. Her thesis had been completed, examined, and her degree awarded.

'I know there's no hope. I accept what the doctors say. But I'd sooner live the rest of my life as Mrs Geddes than Dr Boswell. But he won't hear of it. He says that I must learn to live without him, and that having loved truly once, then I should feel free to love again. How could he? How could he say such a thing?'

'I think he's right. But can you imagine how surprised I am that my brother, of all people, could have turned out to be so wise about something like that? You've changed him. He loves you like I never thought he'd love anyone. No one's loved me like that. Nor have I. Just once, you know, is very, very lucky. And being that sort of person, twice is far from impossible. I think that's what he's telling you, and that for him to marry you when he's so close to dying would be sinfully selfish of him.'

'There would be a legal document revoking my rights to his property. Everything would be left to you.'

'I can't help you, Augusta. I'll do nothing to persuade him. I believe what he says is true. Much as I like you. And I didn't expect to. When he told me of your plans to live here, I felt threatened by them, until I met you and realized what a different man he'd become. You've no idea how sorry I am, and how disappointed I feel about life and what can happen. My father was hardly ever here. He seems to have spent most of his time in the United States. My mother was a confirmed alcoholic by the time I was ten. We were brought up by aunts and tutors, nannies and housekeepers. Has he told you all this?'

'I think I know most of it.'

'I'm so glad you're here, and I wish everything could be different. But I've been wishing for that ever since I could think for myself.'

The weather turned to cloud, rain and starless chill. Augusta Boswell paced the rooms and stairs of her large house cursing the climate for being as black as the Earl of Hell's waistcoat and cold with it. Daphne Geddes's reply was on the telephone answering machine. It had been preserved there for several days. 'Please come and see me as soon as you can,' Daphne's voice said. 'I had to sell Lindorack. I live in a cottage not far from it, though. I had to sell a lot of his books. I didn't have room for them and I needed the money. I couldn't bring myself to tell you because I knew how you'd feel. Can you forgive me? My dear Augusta.' There was a long pause. Augusta could sense the choked hesitancy in Daphne's voice; it felt like a vivid emotion struggling against judgementless, neutral, passive technology. 'Please come soon. I still have his papers and quite a lot of his books.' She repeated her telephone number. It was after midnight, but Augusta picked up the phone and dialled, suspecting that Daphne, too, was a woman for whom sleep was elusive.

Attendance at Erskine's funeral was meagre. The only relatives apart from Daphne were an aunt in her seventies and a slightly younger uncle. Several tenants and employees, a representative of the family's lawyers, and one from the bank, made up the rest of the numbers.

'You can stay for as long as you like,' Daphne said later.

'Just a little while. A cousin and his wife are living in my house in Edinburgh. I've already told them to be out by the end of the month. Harsh, but necessary. They don't understand.'

'Will you look for a job?'

'Universities are about all I'm fit for. Not that there's much demand for what I do.'

'I feel as if I've been orphaned twice over.' Augusta remembered the quiet, puzzled anger in Daphne's voice as she was driven north from Edinburgh. Bridges, motorways, flyovers and speeding cars and trucks made it hard to believe in the early history and customs of the people who once lived on the damaged countryside over which she travelled.

'You seem very calm and determined,' Daphne had said.

'No. It's clear to me that I'll never get what I wanted most. Now it's sunk in, I have to accept that I've no choice but to live without that side to what people call 'happiness'.'

'What ages were your parents when they died?' Daphne asked.

'My father was sixty, and my mother sixty-one. Why do you ask?'

'Not exactly long-lived. My father was forty-four, my mother forty-seven. Erskine was thirty-five. I'm a year older than him. But from an actuarial point of view, my prospects look pretty dire. I'm afraid to ask you to be my friend in case you end up burying me beside Erskine. Or if my presence on a regular footing discourages you from meeting someone else. Men probably find you attractive.'

'You're not exactly plain. And you've got height on your side.'

'Please, stay as long as you like.'

'Just for a little while.'

'I've been wooed,' Daphne said, as if surprised at her disclosure. 'Several times. Chinless wonders, most of them. Awfully good at fly-fishing and from *very* good families, but skint, and good for next to nothing. Am I desperate? Am I frustrated? And to these questions I've had to answer with a truthful, 'No, I'm not.' Sauternes will make me fat, eventually,' she said, 'assuming I get that far.' She examined the bottle. 'Each time I replenish the stocks, I'll think of Erskine and probably cry buckets.'

'He wouldn't drink anything else.'

'What will I put on his stone, Augusta? 'Beloved son of' rings false and horrid.'

'Name, dates, and then 'scholar'.'

'Then 'beloved brother' and 'beloved fiancé'.'

'That's very unusual.'

'I think we should.'

'Yes.'

'Or does it tie a stone around your neck?'

'No. I'm so grateful that my name will be on the stone, too. Thank you.'

'You could hardly have insisted. So, congratulations, me. I've done something thoughtful and unselfish!'

Daphne's cottage was small, the sort of house in which a gardener at Lindorack might have lived, or a gamekeeper. It had a small garden, lazily kept; the house was too close to trees to have other than a darkly cramped outlook. A ladies' bicycle with a large basket before the handlebars lay against a wall beside a rusting rake and an unemptied wheelbarrow full of discoloured weeds. Roses were running wild for lack of pruning, their leaves spotted with lumps of fibrous black. Woodwork looked in need of paint. The porch was dusty. On each side were columns of unused plantpots piled inside each other. The impression was of a demoralized resident within.

They embraced, and Augusta found herself the consoling one, applying her handkerchief to Daphne's tears. 'I have to tell the driver whether to wait, or when, or if, to come back. I thought I'd stay for a few days, if I could, and if you'd like me to,' she said as Daphne shook, wept and nodded. 'Is it all right for me to stay?' Daphne nodded and Augusta went back to the car, told the driver she'd phone his firm in due course, and was handed her suitcase and several boxfiles of papers, which Augusta handed back to the driver, who brought them into the house.

It was six years since they'd last met and visited Erskine's grave. 'There's a lot you'll want to know,' Daphne said. In six years she'd aged markedly. Her appearance wasn't helped by her clothes – a homemade cardigan over a thick polo-necked jumper, a tweed skirt, the waist of which she hitched up every few minutes, ancient ankle-boot slippers which zipped, and wrinkled wool stockings. Her hair was greyer. She looked older than sixty.

'I'd always assumed that the Geddes family fortune was rock solid,' Augusta said. 'I recognize the shelves.'

'I ripped them out. I thought they wouldn't be missed but there was a very nasty letter from their lawyer to my lawyer. I knew I needed shelves, for heaven's sake!'

'You should have told me much, much sooner,' Augusta said.

'I bought it from the Forestry Commission,' Daphne said as Augusta looked at the packed little sitting room. 'I'm not entirely indigent. I've 50,000 left over to provide an income. I can just about get by. I've gin if you'd like a drink.' Augusta looked surprised. 'I don't have any Sauternes.' There was a look in Daphne's eyes which expressed painfully the remorse of someone who knew what she should be providing, but couldn't. 'They didn't have it in the village shop. They'd nothing like that.'

'Don't blame yourself. *I* should have thought of it. I could have brought a case of Sauternes without any trouble.'

'Gin's no good?' The loss of self-confidence was obvious in how Daphne's voice trembled with guilt-ridden timidity.

'I think you've been through sheer hell.'

Daphne shrugged. 'I've had two years to get used to it,' she said lightly. 'I've a room which makes a decent little studio. No central heating, of course, but then Lindorack's was pretty unreliable. Do you remember? And when I think of the bills! I could live for over a year on the likes of that!'

'Have you been all right? I wish you'd *told* me!'

'Please, please, dear Augusta, you really are my only friend, you know. Don't be angry with me! I've been dreading this! It's been like having the guiltiest secret. Sure you won't have gin?'

'Absolutely certain. But what happened?'

'Well, like you I thought everything was taken care of and 100 per cent dependable. Then I'd a letter from the bank saying could their Mr So-and-So come and see me next Wednesday at 11 a.m. and I wrote back saying, 'Yes, fine.' The man came with two briefcases, there was so much paperwork. None of it made sense to me apart from the highly explicit conclusion – *my* share of the Geddes's millions had taken a bad knock.'

'But I read the property supplement in *The Scotsman*. Lindorack wasn't advertised.'

'Naturally. I wouldn't let them. I'd my pride to think of.'

'Didn't you have any warning? I thought you ran the estate yourself.'

'Not the investments. These were what went under. The legal bill for pursuing the chance of mismanagement or something dodgy was *enormous*. Oh, all the estate involved was throwing relatively minor sums of money at it. The blow came out of the blue. Not much pride left now, my dear. None, in fact. But I've settled in quite nicely. I'll have a gin if you won't,' she said with signs of impatience.

'No. Phone a taxi. If your village shop hasn't heard of Sauternes, then we must be able to get it in Dunkeld, surely.' She held Daphne's hand and raised it from the half-empty gin bottle. 'Regular consumer of this stuff, are you?'

'If you're so stuck on Sauternes, then I dare say you're a regular consumer of *that*,' Daphne answered defiantly.

'Very regular. Indeed, practically addicted to it. When I say I drink nothing else, I mean nothing else. Now ring for the taxi.'

After dinner, Daphne said, 'I used to be a competent woman. Now I feel silly and useless. You, though, have become practical.'

'Actually, I think I'm off my rocker.'

'Oh?'

'When the weather's fine I sit in my garden until I'm too pissed to concentrate.'

'Hardly a symptom of madness, whatever else it suggests.'

'I forgot to mention that this occurs between midnight and the early hours. You see, I feel myself to be in very close touch with Erskine, through his books, his handwriting, and the moon and stars.'

'I see,' Daphne said.

'No, you don't 'see'. Nothing occult is behind what I've just said. It's a personal phenomenon to do with the exact physical circumstances which induce the inexplicable but indispensable thrills of a peculiarly intellectual kind of remembrance. And you can believe or disbelieve that as you see fit. Don't ask me to explain it any further because I couldn't do it.'

'All right. If you say so. But I don't understand.'

'The forecast's pretty promising. You'll see for yourself. You might even join me if you're of a mind to.'

'Yes, well, I don't sleep much.'

'I didn't think you did. How much did Hogarth give you for the books?'

'Five hundred.'

'He robbed you. Then he robbed me. Had I known, I'd gladly have bought them from you.'

'What difference does the moon make? I mean, this sitting out that you do. What happens?'

'I don't hear voices, if that's what you're driving at. Nor see visions either. What 'happens' is in here.' She tapped her head. 'Are you really, really sure that you want to live here?'

'But why at *night?*'

'Look, it simply makes a difference. Let's leave it at that. A place like this is too much of a come-down! I don't want to rub it in, Daphne, but the Boswell funds are in a healthy state of growth and my house is too big for two, never mind just me on my ownie-oh. At least, think about it.'

'From Lindorack to charity is worse than from Lindorack to here,' Daphne said.

'Add what you get from selling this dump to your 50,000 and the income would give you all the spending money you need. What I offer is bed, board, and a remarkably efficient cental heating system. To say nothing of the agreeable smell of polished furniture and a relative absence of grime.'

'When we last met you were talking about a professorship. Did you get it?'

'No. They gave it to a world-class halfwit from Oxford with whom I'm at loggerheads. We don't even speak.'

'Why?'

'Because he lives in Oxford and commutes. As well as that, he's a dope. Now, I think living in Edinburgh would be good for you. It might give you a chance to show your work more. You haven't done much about punting your paintings around. Have you?'

'Haven't much felt like it for years. Too many disappointments. I don't know, Augusta. I'm grateful. It's very kind and considerate of you. But I'd like to rest my bones here, beside Erskine.'

'So would I. If it's permissible. If it can be arranged.'

'I couldn't possibly object. And wouldn't. I can fix it.'

'You've no intention of popping off in the near future, I take it?' Augusta asked, suppressing a lady-like Sauternes-repeat.

'I'm a dreadful mess, aren't I? No, I don't feel like dying.'

'Nor me. I've useful work to do,' Augusta said. 'I intend to nag my head of department into a resignation.'

'I don't visit his grave as often as I used to. As often as I should,' Daphne said.

'Isn't it bad for you to live so close to Lindorack and not in it?'

'Well, I see it – rooftops, anyway – when I bike down to the village. Yes, always with a wrench on the old heart-strings. Of course.'

'Very, very acceptable Sauternes,' Augusta said. 'And I'm fussy.'

'Yes, very.'

'If you die first, I'd see to the necessary arrangements, to the letter. I promise. And if I die first . . .'

'I promise, Augusta.'

'And these are promises as readily kept from Edinburgh as here . . .'

'I've said I'll give it serious thought, and I will. You on one side of Erskine, and me on the other. It's only right. It fulfils perfectly what's written on his stone. It makes everything ring true – sad, but true. But maybe not so sad. Anything so true, and loyal, and unforgotten, can't be entirely sad.'

'Personally speaking, I find it miserable beyond words, but, as you say, true, loyal and unforgotten. However, I've lived with it for twenty-five years, so I can grin and bear it for as long as I've got left. But then, I'm that bit younger than you. It's gone midnight and the weather looks quite nice. Shall we sit out?'

They sat on two old chairs on which generations of servants had parked themselves in the kitchens of Lindorack. They held hands and talked about Erskine Gibb Geddes. From time to time Augusta inserted a question or remark to which Daphne replied by saying, 'I'm thinking about it.' After an hour she started to say things like 'I've one of two reservations to clear up with myself, but only I can do that. So why don't you leave me to it?'

'About the only subject on which the lousy schools I was sent to were any good was the stars. One school in particular. I knew all the names. I thought I'd forgotten them, but last month, when I started sitting out, I realized that I hadn't. I seem to have an excellent memory.'

'No one taught the stars to *me*.'

'Erskine knew about them.'

'We always had different tutors.'

Augusta pressed gently on Daphne's hand. 'Think about Erskine.'

'I am.'

'Very soon, it might become moon-blue, silver, starry, and celestial,' Augusta said matter-of-factly. 'But don't be frightened. It's not at all like the Earl of Hell's waistcoat.'

'No,' Daphne said, with a laugh. 'Not at all.'

'But first, I want to make a toast,' Augusta said tipsily, in her won't-take-no-for-an-answer manner.

'A toast?'

'To the sky.'

'To the sky!'

'To the sky!'

And the moon giggled, having seen everything, not once, but many times.